Father Stafford

Anthony Hope

FATHER STAFFORD

BY

ANTHONY HOPE

AUTHOR OF "A MAN OF MARK," "THE PRISONER OF ZENDA."

F. TENNYSON NEELY
PUBLISHER
CHICAGO NEW YORK
1895

CONTENTS.

CHAPTER I.

Eugene Lane and his Guests.

The world considered Eugene Lane a very fortunate young man; and if youth, health, social reputation, a seat in Parliament, a large income, and finally the promised hand of an acknowledged beauty can make a man happy, the world was right. It is true that Sir Roderick Ayre had been heard to pity the poor chap on the ground that his father had begun life in the workhouse; but everybody knew that Sir Roderick was bound to exalt the claims of birth, inasmuch as he had to rely solely upon them for a reputation, and discounted the value of his opinion accordingly. After all, it was not as if the late Mr. Lane had ended life in the undesirable shelter in question. On the contrary, his latter days had been spent in the handsome mansion of Millstead Manor; and, as he lay on his deathbed, listening to the Rector's gentle homily on the vanity of riches, his eyes would wander to the window and survey a wide tract of land that he called his own, and left, together with immense sums of money, to his son, subject only to a jointure for his wife. It is hard to blame the tired old man if he felt, even with the homily ringing in his ears, that he had not played his part in the world badly.

Millstead Manor was indeed the sort of place to raise a doubt as to the utter vanity of riches. It was situated hard by the little village of Millstead, that lies some forty miles or so northwest of London, in the middle of rich country. The neighborhood afforded shooting, fishing, and hunting, if not the best of their kind, yet good enough to satisfy reasonable people. The park was large and well wooded; the house had insisted on remaining picturesque in spite of Mr. Lane's improvements, and by virtue of an indelible stamp of antiquity had carried its point. A house that dates from Elizabeth is not to be entirely put to shame by one or two unblushing French windows and other trifling barbarities of that description, more especially when it is kept in countenance by a little church of still greater age, nestling under its wing in a manner that recalled the good old days when the lord of the manor was lord of the souls and bodies of his tenants. Even old Mr. Lane had been mellowed by the influence of his new home, and before his death had come to play the part of Squire far more respectably than might be imagined. Eugene sustained the *rôle* with the graceful indolence and careless efficiency that marked most of his doings.

He stood one Saturday morning in the latter part of July on the steps that led from the terrace to the lawn, holding a letter in his hand and softly whistling. In appearance he was not, it must be admitted, an ideal Squire, for he was but a trifle above middle height, rather slight, and with the little stoop that tells of the man who is town-bred and by nature more given to indoor than outdoor exercises; but he was a good-looking fellow for all that, with a bright humorous face,—though at this moment rather a bored one,—large eyes set well apart, and his proper allowance of brown hair and white teeth. Altogether, it may safely be said that, not even Sir Roderick's nose could have sniffed the workhouse in the young master of Millstead Manor.

Still whistling, Eugene descended the steps and approached a group of people sitting under a large copper-beech tree. A still, hot summer morning does not incline the mind or the body to activity, and all of them had sunk into attitudes of ease. Mrs. Lane's work was reposing in her lap; her sister, Miss Jane Chambers, had ceased the pretense of reading; the Rector was enjoying what he kept assuring himself was only just five minutes' peace before he crossed over to his parsonage and his sermon; Lady Claudia Territon and Miss Katharine Bernard were each in possession of a wicker lounge, while at their feet lay two young men in flannels, with lawn-tennis racquets lying idle by them. A large jug of beer close to the elbow of one of them completed the luxurious picture that was framed in a light cloud of tobacco smoke, traceable to the person who also was obviously responsible for the beer.

As Eugene approached, a sudden thought seemed to strike him. He stopped deliberately, and with great care lit a cigar.

"Why wasn't I smoking, I wonder!" he said. "The sight of Bob Territon reminded me." Then as he reached them, raising his voice, he went on:

"Ladies and gentlemen, I am sorry to interrupt you, and with bad news."

"What is the matter, dear," asked Mrs. Lane, a gentle old lady, who having once had the courage to leave the calm of her father's country vicarage to follow the doubtful fortunes of her husband, was now reaping her reward in a luxury of which she had never dreamed.

"With the arrival of the 4.15 this afternoon," Eugene continued, "our placid life will be interrupted, and one of Mr. Eugene Lane, M.P.'s, celebrated Saturday to Monday parties (I quote from *The Universe*) will begin."

"Who's coming?" asked Miss Bernard.

Miss Bernard was the acknowledged beauty referred to in the opening lines of this chapter, whose love Eugene had been lucky enough to secure. Had Eugene not been absurdly rich himself, he might have been congratulated further on the prospective enjoyment of a nice little fortune as well as the lady's favor.

"Is Rickmansworth coming?" put in Lady Claudia, before Eugene had time to reply to his *fiancée*.

"Be at peace," he said, addressing Lady Claudia; "your brother is not coming. I have known Rickmansworth a long while, and I never knew him to be polite. He inquired by telegram (reply not paid) who were to be here. When I wired him, telling him whom I had the privilege of entertaining, and requesting an immediate reply (not paid), he answered that he thought I must have enough Territons already, and he didn't want to make another."

Neither Lady Claudia nor her brother Robert, who was the young man with the beer, seemed put out at this message. Indeed, the latter went so far as to say:

"Good! Have some beer, Eugene?"

"But who is coming?" repeated Miss Kate. "Really, Eugene, you might pay a little attention to me."

"Can't, my dear Kate—not in public. It's not good form, is it, Lady Claudia?"

"Eugene," said Mrs. Lane, in a tone as nearly severe as she ever arrived at, "if you wish your guests to have either dinner or beds, you will at once tell me who and how many they are."

"My dear mother, they are in number five, composed as follows: First, the Bishop of Bellminster."

"A most interesting man," observed Miss Chambers.

"I am glad to hear it, Aunt Jane," responded Eugene. "The Bishop is accompanied by his wife. That makes two; and then old Merton, who was at the Colonial Office you know, and Morewood the painter make four."

"Sir George Merton is a Radical, isn't he?" asked Lady Claudia severely.

"He tries to be," said Eugene. "Shall I order a carriage to take you to the station? I think, you know, you can stand it, with Haddington's help."

Mr. Spencer Haddington, the other young man in flannels, was a very rising member of the Conservative party, of which Lady Claudia conceived herself to be a pillar. Identity of political views, in Mr. Haddington's opinion, might well pave the way to a closer union, and this hope accounted for his having consented to pair with Eugene, who sat on the other side, and spend the last week in idleness at Millstead.

"Well," said Mr. Robert Territon, "it sounds slow, old man."

"Candid family, the Territons," remarked Eugene to the copper-beech.

"Who's the fifth? you've only told us four," said Kate, who always stuck to the point.

"The fifth is—" Eugene paused a moment, as though preparing a sensation; "the fifth is—Father Stafford."

Now it was a remarkable thing that all the ladies looked up quickly and re-echoed the name of the last guest in accents of awe, whereas the men seemed unaffected.

"Why, where did you pick *him* up?" asked Lady Claudia.

"Pick him up! I've known Charley Stafford since we were both that high. We were at Harrow and at Oxford together. Rickmansworth knows him, Bob. You didn't come till he'd left."

"Why is the gentleman called 'Father'?" said Bob.

"Because he is a priest," Miss Chambers answered. "And really, Mr. Territon, you're very ignorant. Everybody knows Father Stafford. You do, Mr. Haddington?"

"Yes," said Haddington, "I've heard of him. He's an Anglican Father, isn't he? Had a big parish somewhere down the Mile End Road?"

"Yes," said Eugene. "He's an old and a great friend of mine. He's quite knocked up, poor old chap, and had to get leave of absence; and I've made him promise to come and stay here for a good part of the time, to rest."

"Then he's not going off again on Monday?" asked Mrs. Lane.

"Oh, I hope not. He's writing a book or something, that will keep him from being restless."

"How charming!" said Lady Claudia. "Don't you dote on him, Kate? Please, Mr. Lane, may I stay too?"

"By the way," said Eugene, "Stafford has taken a vow of celibacy."

"I knew that," said Lady Claudia imperturbably.

Eugene looked mournful; Bob Territon groaned tragically; but Lady Claudia was quite unmoved, and, turning to the Rector, who sat smiling benevolently on the young people, asked:

"Do you know Father Stafford, Dr. Dennis?"

"No. I should be much interested in meeting him. I've heard so much of his work and his preaching."

"Yes," said Lady Claudia, "and his penances and fasting, and so on."

"Poor old Stafford!" said Eugene. "It's quite enough for him that a thing's pleasant to make it wrong."

"Not your philosophy, Master Eugene!" said the Rector.

"No, Doctor."

"But what's this vow?" asked Kate.

"There's no such thing as a binding vow of celibacy in the Anglican Church," announced Miss Chambers.

"Is that right, Doctor?" said Lady Claudia.

"God bless me, my dear," said the Rector, "I don't know. There wasn't in my time."

"But, Eugene, surely I'm right," persisted Aunt Jane. "His Bishop can dispense him from it, can't he?"

"Don't know," answered Eugene. "He says he can."

"Who says he can?"

"Why, the Bishop!"

"Well, then, of course he can."

"All right," said Eugene; "only Stafford doesn't think so. Not that he wants to be released. He doesn't care a bit about women—very ungrateful, as they're all mad about him."

"That's very rude, Eugene," said Kate, in reproving tones. "Admiration for a saint is not madness. Shall we go in, Claudia, and leave these men to pipes and beer?"

"One for you, Rector!" chuckled Bob Territon, who knew no reverence.

The two girls departed somewhat scornfully, arm in arm, and the Rector too rose with a sigh, and accompanied the elder ladies to the house, whither they were going to meet the pony carriage that stood at the hall door. A daily drive was part of Mrs. Lane's ritual.

"By the way, you fellows," Eugene resumed, throwing himself on the grass, "I may as well mention that Stafford doesn't drink, or eat meat, or smoke, or play cards, or anything else."

"What a peculiar beggar!" said Bob.

"Yes, and he's peculiar in another way," said Eugene, a little dryly; "he particularly objects to any remark being made on his habits—I mean on what he eats and drinks and so on."

"There I agree," said Bob; "I object to any remarks on what I eat and drink"; and he look a long pull at the beer.

"You must treat him with respect, young man. Haddington, I know, will study him as a phenomenon. I can't protect him against that."

Mr. Haddington smiled and remarked that such revivals of mediævalism were interesting, if morbid; and having so delivered himself, he too went his way.

"That chap's considered very clever, isn't he?" asked Bob of his host, indicating Haddington's retreating figure.

"Very, I believe," said Eugene. "He's a cuckoo, you see."

"Dashed if I do," said Bob.

"He steals other birds' nests—eggs and all."

"Your natural history is a trifle mixed, old fellow; kindly explain."

"Well, he's a thief of ideas. Never was the father of one himself, and gets his living by kidnapping."

"I never knew such a chap!" ejaculated Bob helplessly. "Why can't you say plainly that you think he's an ass?"

"I don't," said Eugene. "He's by no means an ass. He's a very clever fellow. But he lives on other men's ideas!"

"Oh! come and play billiards."

"I can't," said Eugene gravely. "I'm going to read poetry to Kate."

"By Jove, does she make you do that?"

Eugene nodded sadly, and Bob went off into a fit of obtrusive chuckling. Eugene cast a large cushion dexterously at him and caught him just in the mouth, and, still sadly, rose and went in search of his lady-love.

"Why the dickens does he marry that girl?" exclaimed Bob. "It beats me."

Bob Territon was not the only person in whom Eugene's engagement to Kate Bernard inspired some surprise. But neither he nor any one else succeeded in formulating very definite reasons for the feeling. Kate was a beauty, and a beauty of a type undeniably orthodox and almost aristocratic. She was tall and slight, her nose was the least trifle arched, her fingers tapered, and so, it was believed, did her feet. Her hair was golden, her mouth was small, and her accomplishments considerable. From her childhood she had been considered clever, and had vindicated her reputation by gaining more than one certificate from the various examining bodies which nowadays go up and down seeking whom they may devour. All these varied excellences Eugene had had full opportunities of appreciating, for Kate was a distant cousin of his on the mother's side, and had spent a large part of the last few years at the Manor. It was, in fact, so obviously the duty of the two young people to fall in love with one another, that the surprise exhibited by their friends could only have been based on a somewhat cynical view of humanity. The cynics ought to have considered themselves confuted by the *fait accompli*, but they refused to do so, and, led by Sir Roderick Ayre, had been known to descend to laying five to four against the permanency of the engagement—an obviously coarse and improper proceeding.

It is possible that the odds might have risen a point or two, had these reprehensible persons been present at the little scene which occurred on the terrace, whither the girls had betaken themselves, and Eugene in his turn repaired when he had armed himself with Tennyson. As he approached Claudia rose to go and leave the lovers to themselves.

"Don't go, Lady Claudia," said Eugene. "I'm not going to read anything you ought not to hear."

Of course it was the right thing for Claudia to go, and she knew it. But she was a mischievous body, and the sight of a cloud on Kate's brow had upon her exactly the opposite effect to what it ought to have had.

"You don't really want me to stay, do you? Wouldn't you two rather be alone?" she asked.

"Much rather have you," Eugene answered.

Kate rose with dignity.

"We need not discuss that," she said. "I have letters to write, and am going indoors."

"Oh, I say, Kate, don't do that! I came out on purpose to read to you."

"Lady Claudia is quite ready to make an audience for you," was the chilling reply, as Kate vanished through the open door.

"There, you've done it now!" said Eugene. "You really ought not to insist on staying."

"I'm so sorry, Mr. Lane. But it's all your fault." And Claudia tried to make her face assume a look of gravity.

A pause ensued, and then they both smiled.

"What were you going to read?" asked Claudia.

"Oh, Tennyson—always read Tennyson. Kate likes it, because she thinks it's simple."

"You flatter yourself that you see the deeper meaning?"

Eugene smiled complacently.

"And you mean Kate doesn't? I'm glad I'm not engaged to you, Mr. Lane, if that's the kind of thing you say."

Eugene opened his mouth, shut it again, and then said blandly:

"So am I."

"Thank you! You need not be afraid."

"If I were engaged to you, I mightn't like you so well."

A slight blush became visible on Claudia's usually pale cheek.

Eugene looked away toward the horizon.

"I like the way quite pale people blush," he said.

"What do you want, Mr. Lane?"

"Ah! I see you appreciate my character. I want many things I can't have—a great many."

"No doubt," said Claudia, still blushing under the mournful gaze which accompanied those words. "Do you want anything you can have?"

"Yes! I want you to stay several more weeks."

"I'm going to stay." said Claudia.

"How kind!" exclaimed Eugene.

"Do you know why?"

"My modesty forbids me to think."

"I want, to see a lot of Father Stafford! Good-by, Mr. Lane. I'll leave you to your private and particular understanding of Tennyson."

"Claudia!"

"Hold your tongue," she whispered, in tones of exasperation. "It's very wicked and very impertinent—and the library door's open, and Kate's in there!"

Eugene fell back in his chair with a horrified look, and Claudia rushed into the house.

CHAPTER II.

New Faces and Old Feuds.

There was, no doubt, some excuse for the interest that the ladies at Millstead Manor had betrayed on hearing the name of Father Stafford. In these days, when the discussion of theological topics has emerged from the study into the street, there to jostle persons engaged in their lawful business, a man who makes for himself a position as a prominent champion of any view becomes, to a considerable extent, a public character; and Charles Stafford's career had excited much notice. Although still a young man but little past thirty, he was adored by a powerful body of followers, and received the even greater compliment of hearty detestation from all, both within and without the Church, to whom his views seemed dangerous and pernicious. He had administered a large parish with distinction; he had written a treatise of profound patristic learning and uncompromising sacerdotal pretensions. He had defended the institution of a celibate priesthood, and was known to have treated the Reformation with even less respect than it has been of late accustomed to receive. He had done more than all this: he had impressed all who met him with a character of absolute devotion and disinterestedness, and there were many who thought that a successor to the saints might be found in Stafford, if anywhere in this degenerate age. Yet though he was, or was thought to be, all this, his friends were yet loud in declaring—and ever foremost among them Eugene Lane—that a better, simpler, or more modest man did not exist. For the weakness of humanity, it may be added that Stafford's appearance gave him fully the external aspect most suitable to the part his mind urged him to play; for he was tall and spare; his fine-cut face, clean shaven, displayed the penetrating eyes, prominent nose, and large mobile mouth that the memory associates with pictures of Italian prelates who were also statesmen. These personal characteristics, combined with his attitude on Church matters, caused him to be familiarly known among the flippant by the nickname of the Pope.

Eugene Lane stood upon his hearthrug, conversing with the Bishop of Bellminster and covertly regarding his betrothed out of the corner of an apprehensive eye. They had not met alone since the morning, and he was naturally anxious to find out whether that unlucky "Claudia" had been overheard. Claudia herself was listening to the conversation of Mr. Morewood, the well-known artist; and Stafford, who had only arrived just before dinner, was still busy in answering Mrs. Lane's questions about his health. Sir George Merton had failed at the last moment, "like a Radical," said Claudia.

"I am extremely interested in meeting your friend Father Stafford," said the Bishop.

"Well, he's a first-rate fellow," replied Eugene. "I'm sure you'll like him."

"You young fellows call him the Pope, don't you?" asked his lordship, who was a genial man.

"Yes. You don't mind, do you? It's not as if we called him the Archbishop of Canterbury, you know."

"I shouldn't consider even that very personal," said the Bishop, smiling.

Dinner was announced. Eugene gave the Bishop's wife his arm, whispering to Claudia as he passed, "Age before impudence"; and that young lady found that she had fallen to the lot of Stafford, whereat she was well pleased. Kate was paired with Haddington, and Mr. Morewood with Aunt Jane. The Bishop, of course, escorted the hostess.

"And who," said he, almost as soon as he was comfortably settled to his soup, "is the young lady sitting by our friend the Father—the one, I mean, with dark hair, not Miss Bernard? I know her."

"That's Lady Claudia Territon," said Mrs. Lane. "Very pretty, isn't she? and really a very good girl."

"Do you say 'really' because, unless you did, I shouldn't believe it?" he asked, with a smile.

Mrs. Lane had been moved by this idea, but not consciously and, a little distressed at suspecting herself of an unkindness, entertained the Bishop with an entirely fanciful catalogue of Claudia's virtues, which, being overheard by Bob Territon, who had no lady, and was at liberty to listen, occasioned him immense entertainment.

Claudia, meanwhile, was drifting into a state of some annoyance. Stafford was very courteous and attentive, but he drank nothing, and apparently proposed to dine off dry bread. When she began to question him about his former parish, instead of showing the gratitude that might be expected, he smiled a smile that she found pleasure in describing as inscrutable, and said:

"Please don't talk down to me, Lady Claudia."

"I have been taught," responded Claudia, rather stiffly, "to talk about subjects in which my company is presumably interested."

Stafford looked at her with some surprise. It must be admitted that he had become used to more submission than Claudia seemed inclined to give him.

"I beg your pardon. You are quite right. Let us talk about it."

"No, I won't. We will talk about you. You've been very ill, Father Stafford?"

"A little knocked up."

"I don't wonder!" she said, with an irritated glance at his plate, which was now furnished with a potato.

He saw the glance.

"It wasn't that," he said; "that suits me very well."

Claudia knew that a pretty girl may say most things, so she said:

"I don't believe it. You're killing yourself. Why don't you do as the Bishop does?"

The Bishop, good man, was at this moment drinking champagne.

"Men have different ways of living," he answered evasively.

"I think yours is a very bad way. Why do you do it?"

"I'm sure you will forgive me if I decline to discuss the question just now. I notice you take a little wine. You probably would not care to explain why."

"I take it because I like it."

"And I don't take it because I like it."

Claudia had a feeling that she was being snubbed, and her impression was confirmed when Stafford, a moment afterward, turned to Kate Bernard, who sat on his left hand, and was soon deep in reminiscences of old visits to the Manor, with which Kate contrived to intermingle a little flattery that Stafford recognized only to ignore. They had known one another well in earlier days, and Kate was immensely pleased at finding her playfellow both famous and not forgetful.

Eugene looked on from his seat at the foot of the table with silent wonder. Here was a man who might and indeed ought to talk to Claudia, and yet was devoting himself to Kate.

"I suppose it's on the same principle that he takes water instead of champagne," he thought; but the situation amused him, and he darted at Claudia a look that conveyed to that young lady the urgent idea that she was, as boys say, "dared" to make Father Stafford talk to her. This was quite enough. Helped by the unconscious alliance of Haddington, who thought Miss Bernard had let him alone quite long enough, she seized her opportunity, and said in the softest voice:

"Father Stafford?"

Stafford turned his head, and found fixed upon him a pair of large, dark eyes, brimming over with mingled contrition and admiration.

"I am so sorry—but—but I thought you looked so ill."

Stafford was unpleasantly conscious of being human. The triumph of wickedness is a spectacle from which we may well avert our eyes.

Suffice it to say that a quarter of an hour later Claudia returned Eugene's glance with a look of triumph and scorn.

Meanwhile, trouble had arisen between the Bishop and Mr. Morewood. Morewood was an artist of great ability, originality, and skill; and if he had not attained the honors of the Academy, it was perhaps more of his own fault than that of the exalted body in question, as he always treated it with an ostentatious contumely. After all, the Academy must be allowed its feelings. Moreover, his opinions on many subjects were known to be extreme, and he was not chary of displaying them. He was sitting on Mrs. Lane's left, opposite the Bishop, and the latter had started with his hostess a discussion of the relation between religion and art. All went harmoniously for a time; they agreed that religion had ceased to inspire art, and that it was a very regrettable thing; and there, one would have thought the subject—not being a new one—might well have been left. Suddenly, however, Mr. Morewood broke in:

"Religion has ceased to inspire art because it has lost its own inspiration, and having so ceased, it has lost its only use."

The Bishop was annoyed. A well-bred man himself, he disliked what seemed to him ill-bred attacks on opinions which his position proclaimed him to hold.

"You cannot expect me to assent to either of your propositions, Mr. Morewood," he said. "If I believed them, you know, I should not be in the place I am."

"They're true, for all that," retorted Morewood. "And what is it to be traced to?"

"I'm sure I don't know," said poor Mrs. Lane.

"Why, to Established Churches, of course. As long as fancies and imaginary beings are left free to each man to construct or destroy as he will,—or again, I may say, as long as they are fluid,—they subserve the pleasurableness of life. But when you take in hand and make a Church out of them, and all that, what can you expect?"

"I think you must be confusing the Church with the Royal Academy," observed the Bishop, with some acidity.

"There would be plenty of excuse for me, if I did," replied Morewood. "There's no truth and no zeal in either of them."

"If you please, we will not discuss the truth. But as to the zeal, what do you say to the example of it among us now?" And the Bishop, lowering his voice, indicated Stafford.

Morewood directed a glance at him.

"He's mad!" he said briefly.

"I wish there were a few more with the same mania about."

"You don't believe all he does?"

"Perhaps I can't see all he does," said the Bishop, with a touch of sadness.

"How do you mean?"

"I have been longer in the cave, and perhaps I have peered too much through cave-spectacles."

Morewood looked at him for a moment.

"I'm sorry if I've been rude, Bishop," he said more quietly, "but a man must say what he thinks."

"Not at all times," said the Bishop; and he turned pointedly to Mrs. Lane and began to discuss indifferent matters.

Morewood looked round with a discontented air. Miss Chambers was mortally angry with him and had turned to Bob Territon, whom she was trying to persuade to come to a bazaar at Bellminster on the Monday. Bob was recalcitrant, and here too the atmosphere became a little disturbed. The only people apparently content were Kate and Haddington and Lady Claudia and Stafford. To the rest it was a relief when Mrs. Lane gave the signal to rise.

Matters improved, however, in the drawing-room. The Bishop and Stafford were soon deep in conversation; and Claudia, thus deprived of her former companion, condescended to be very gracious to Mr. Morewood, in the secret hope that that eccentric genius would make her the talk of the studios next summer by painting her portrait. Haddington and Bob had vanished with cigars; and Eugene looking round and seeing that all was peace, said to himself in an access of dutifulness. "Now for it!" and crossed over to where Kate sat, and invited her to accompany him into the garden.

Kate acquiesced, but showed little other sign of relaxing her attitude of lofty displeasure. She left Eugene to begin.

"I'm awfully sorry, Kate, if you were vexed this morning."

Absolute silence.

"But, you see, as host here, I couldn't very well turn out Lady Claudia."

"Why don't you say Claudia?" asked Kate, in sarcastic tones.

Eugene felt inclined to fly, but he recognized that his only chance lay in pretending innocence when he had it not.

"Are we to quarrel about a trifle of that sort?" he asked; "a girl I've known like a sister for the last ten years!"

Kate smiled bitterly.

"Do you really suppose that deceives me? Of course I am not afraid of your falling in love with Claudia; but it's very bad taste to have anything at all like flirtation with her."

"Quite right; it is. It shall not occur again. Isn't that enough?"

Kate, in spite of her confidence, was not anxious to drive Eugene with too tight a rein, so, with a nearer approach to graciousness she allowed it to appear that it was enough.

"Then come along," he said, passing his arm around her waist, and running her briskly along the terrace to a seat at the end, where he deposited her.

"Really, Eugene, one would think you were a schoolboy. Suppose any one had seen us!"

"Some one did," said Eugene composedly, lighting his cigar.

"Who?"

"Haddington. He was sitting on the step of the sun-dial, smoking."

"*How* annoying! What's he doing there?"

"If you ask me, I expect he's waiting on the chance of Lady Claudia coming out."

"I should think it very unlikely," said Kate, with an impatient tap of her foot; "and I wish you wouldn't do such things."

Eugene smiled; and having thus, as he conceived, partly avenged himself, devoted the next ten minutes to orthodox love-making, with the warmth of which Kate had no reason to be discontent. On the expiration of that time he pleaded his obligations as a host, and they returned to the house, Kate much mollified, Eugene with the peaceful but fatigued air that tells of duty done.

Before going to bed, Stafford and Eugene managed to get a few words together. Leaving the other men, except the Bishop, who was already at rest, in the billiard-room, they strolled out together on to the terrace.

"Well, old man, how are you getting on?" asked Eugene.

"Capitally! stronger every day in body and happier in mind. I grumbled a great deal when I first broke down, but now I'm not sure a rest isn't good for me. You can stop and have a look where you are going to."

"And you think you can stand it?"

"Stand what, my dear fellow?"

"Why, the life you lead—a life studiously emptied of everything that makes life pleasant."

"Ah! you are like Lady Claudia!" said Stafford, smiling. "I can tell you, though, what I can hardly tell her. There are some men who can make no terms with the body. Does that sound very mediæval? I mean men who, unless they are to yield utterly to pleasure, must have no dealings with it."

"You boycott pleasure for fear of being too fond of it?"

"Yes; I don't lay down that rule for everybody. For me it is the right and only one."

"You think it right for a good many people, though?"

"Well, you know, the many-headed beast is strong."

"For me?"

"Wait till I get at you from the pulpit."

"No; tell me now."

"Honestly?"

"Of course! I take that for granted."

"Well, then, old fellow," said he, laying a hand on Eugene's arm, with a slight gesture of caress not unusual with him, "in candor and without unkindness, yes!"

"I could never do it," said Eugene.

"Perhaps not—or, at least, not yet."

"Too late or too early, is it?"

"It may be so, but I will not say so."

"You know I think you're all wrong?"

"I know."

"You will fail."

"God forbid! but if he pleases—"

"After all, what are meat, wine, and—and so on for?"

"That argument is beneath you, Eugene."

"So it is. I beg your pardon. I might as well ask what the hangman is for if nobody is to be hanged. However, I'm determined that you shall enjoy yourself for a week here, whether you like it or not."

Stafford smiled gently and bade him good-night. A moment later Bob Territon emerged from the open windows of the billiard-room.

"Of all dull dogs, Haddington's the worst; however, I've won five pound of him! Hist! Is the Father here?"

"I am glad to say he is not."

"Oh! Have you squared it with Miss Kate? I saw something was up."

"Miss Bernard's heart, Bob, and mine again beat as one."

"What was it particularly about?"

"An immaterial matter."

"I say, did you see the Father and Claudia?"

"No. What do you mean?"

"Gammon! I tell you what, Eugene, if Claudia really puts her back into it, I wouldn't give much for that vow of celibacy."

"Bob," said Eugene, "you don't know Stafford; and your expression about your sister is—well, shall I say lacking in refinement?"

"Haddington didn't like it."

"Damn Haddington, and you too!" said Eugene impatiently, walking away.

Bob looked after him with a chuckle, and exclaimed enigmatically to the silent air, "Six to four, t. and o."

CHAPTER III.

Father Stafford changes his Habits, and Mr. Haddington his Views.

For sheer placid enjoyment and pleasantness of living, there is nothing like a sojourn in a well-appointed country house, peopled by well-assorted guests. The guests at Millstead Manor were not perhaps particularly well-assorted; but nevertheless the hours passed by in a round of quiet delights, and the long summer days seemed in no wise tedious. The Bishop and Mrs. Bartlett had reluctantly gone to open the bazaar, and Miss Chambers went with them, but otherwise the party was unchanged; for Morewood, who had come originally only for two days, had begged leave to stay, received it on condition of showing due respect to everybody's prejudices, telegraphed for his materials, and was fitfully busy making sketches, not of Lady Claudia, to her undisguised annoyance, but of Stafford, with whose face he had been wonderfully struck. Stafford himself was the only one of the party, besides his artistic tormentor, who had not abandoned himself to the charms of idleness. His great work was understood to make rapid progress between six in the morning, when he always rose, and half-past nine, when the party assembled at breakfast; and he was also busy in writing a reply to a daring person who had recently asserted in print that on the whole the less said about the Council of Chalcedon the better.

"The Pope's wild about it!" reported Bob Territon to the usual after-breakfast group on the lawn: "says the beggar's impudence licks him."

"He shall not work any more," exclaimed Claudia, darting into the house, whence she presently emerged, followed by Stafford, who resignedly sat himself down with them.

Such forcible interruptions of his studies were by no means uncommon. Eugene, however, who was of an observant turn, noticed—and wondered if others did—that the raids on his seclusion were much more apt to be successful when Claudia headed them

23

than under other auspices. The fact troubled him, not only from certain unworthy feelings which he did his best to suppress, but also because he saw nothing but harm to be possible from any close *rapprochement* between Claudia and Stafford. Kate, on the contrary, seemed to him to have set herself the task of throwing them together; with what motive he could not understand, unless it were the recollection of his ill-fated "Claudia." He did not think this explanation very convincing, for he was well aware that Kate's scorn of Claudia's attractions, as compared with her own, was perfectly genuine, and such a state of mind would not produce the certainly active efforts she put forth. In truth, Eugene, though naturally observant, was, like all men, a little blind where he himself was concerned; and perhaps a shrewd spectator would have connected Haddington in some way with Miss Kate's maneuvers. Such, at any rate, was the view of Bob Territon, and no doubt he would have expressed it with his usual frankness if he had not had his own reasons for keeping silence.

Stafford's state of mind was somewhat peculiar. A student from his youth, to whom invisible things had always seemed more real than visible, and hours of solitude better filled than busy days, he had had but little experience of that sort of humanity among which he found himself. A man may administer a cure of souls with marked efficiency in the Mile End Road, and yet find himself much at a loss when confronted with the latest products of the West End. The renunciation of the world, except so far as he could aid in mending it, had seemed an easy and cheap price to pay for the guerdon he strove for, to one who had never seen how pleasant this wicked world can look in certain of its aspects. Hitherto, at school, at college, and afterward, he had resolutely turned away from all opportunities of enlarging his experience in this direction. He had shunned society, and had taken great pains to restrict his acquaintance with the many devout ladies who had sought him out to the barest essentials of what ought to have been, if it was not always, their purpose in seeking him. The prince of this world was now preparing a more subtle attack; and under the seeming compulsion of common prudence no less than of old friendship, he found himself flung into the very center of the sort of life he had with such pains avoided. It may be doubted whether he was not, like an unskillful swimmer, ignorant of his danger; but it is certain that, had he been able to search out his own heart with his former acuteness of self-judgment, he would have found the first germs of inclinations and feelings to which he had been up till now a stranger. He would have discovered the birth of a new longing for pleasure, a growing delight in the sensuous side of things; or rather, he would have become convinced that temptations of this sort, which had previously been in the main creatures of his own brain, postulated in obedience to the doctrines and literature in which he had been bred, had become self-assertive realities; and that what had been set up only to be triumphantly knocked down had now taken a strong root of its own, and refused to be displaced by spiritual exercises or physical mortifications. Had he been able to pursue the analysis yet further, it may be that, even in these days, he would have found that the forces of this world were already beginning to personify themselves for him in the attractive figure of Claudia Territon. As it was, however, this discovery was yet far from him.

The function of passing a moral judgment on Claudia's conduct at this juncture is one that the historian respectfully declines. It is easy to blame fair damsels for recklessness in the use of their dangerous weapons; and if they take the censure to heart—which is not usually the case—easy again to charge them with self-consciousness or self-conceit. We do not know their temptations and may not presume to judge them. And it may well be thought that Claudia would have been guilty of an excessive appreciation of herself had her conduct been influenced by the thought that such a man as Stafford was likely to fall in love with her. Of the conscious design of attracting him she must be acquitted, for she acted under the force of a strong attraction exercised by him. Her mind was not entirely engrossed in the pleasures, and what she imagined to be the duties, of her station. She had a considerable, if untrained and erratic, instinct toward religion, and exhibited that leaning toward the mysterious and visionary which is the common mark of an acute mind that has not been presented with any methodical course of training worthy of its abilities. Such a temperament could not fail to be powerfully influenced by Stafford; and when an obvious and creditable explanation lies on the surface, it is an ungracious task to probe deeper in the hope of coming to something less praiseworthy.

Claudia herself certainly undertook no such research. It was not her habit to analyze her motives; and, if asked the reasons of her conduct, she would no doubt have replied that she sought Stafford because she liked him. Perhaps, if further pressed, she would have admitted that she found him occasionally a useful refuge against attentions from two other quarters which she found it necessary to avoid; in the one case because she would have liked them, in the other for exactly the opposite reason.

It cannot, however, be supposed that this latter line of diplomacy could be permanently successful. When you only meet your suitor at dances or operas, it may be no hard task to be always surrounded by a *chevaux-de-frise* of other admirers. We have all seen that maneuver brilliantly and patiently executed. But when you are staying at a country house with any man of average pertinacity, I make bold to say that nothing short of taking to bed can be permanently relied upon. If this is the case with the ordinary man, how much more does it hold good when the assailant is one like Haddington—a man of considerable address, unbounded persistence, and limitless complacency? There came a time when Claudia's forced marches failed her, and she had to turn and give battle. When the moment came she was prepared with an audacious plan of campaign.

She had walked down to the village one morning, attended by Haddington and protected by Bob, to buy for Mrs. Lane a fresh supply of worsted wool, a commodity apparently necessary to sustain that lady's life, and was returning at peace, when Bob suddenly exclaimed:

"By Jove! Tobacco! Wait for me!" and, turning, fled back whence he came, at full speed.

Claudia made an attempt at following him, but the weather was hot and the road dusty, and, confronted with the alternative of a *tête-à-tête* and a damaged personal appearance, she reluctantly chose the former.

Haddington did not let the grass grow under his feet. "Well," he said, "it won't be unpleasant to rest a little while, will it? Here's a dry bank."

Claudia never wasted time in dodging the inevitable. She sat down.

"I am very glad of this opportunity," Haddington began, in such a tone as a man might use if he had just succeeded in moving the adjournment. "It's curious how little I have managed to see of you lately, Lady Claudia."

"We meet at least five times a day, Mr. Haddington—breakfast, lunch, tea—"

"I mean when you are alone."

"Oh!"

"And yet you must know my great—my only object in being here is to see you."

"The less I say the sooner it will be over," thought Claudia, whose experience was considerable.

"You must have noticed my—my attachment. I hope it was without displeasure?"

This clearly called for an answer, but Claudia gave none. She sighed slightly and put up her parasol.

"Claudia, is there any hope for me? I love you more—"

"Mr. Haddington," said Claudia, "this is a painful scene. I trust nothing in my conduct has misled you. [This was known—how, I do not know—to her brothers as "Claudia's formula," but it is believed not to be uncommon.] But what you propose is utterly impossible."

"Why do you say that? Perhaps you do not know me well enough yet—but in time, surely?"

"Mr. Haddington," said Claudia, "let me speak plainly. Even if I loved you—which I don't and never shall, for immense admiration for a man's abilities is a different thing from love [Haddington looked somewhat soothed], I could never consent to accept the position of a *pis-aller*. That is not the Territon way." And Lady Claudia looked very proud.

"A *pis-aller*! What in the world do you mean?"

"Girls are not supposed to see anything. But do you think I imagine you would ever have honored me in this way unless a greater prize had been—had appeared to be out of reach?"

This was not fair; but it was near enough to the mark to make Haddington a little uneasy. Had Kate been free, he would certainly have been in doubt.

"I bear no malice about that," she continued, smiling, "only you mustn't pretend to be broken-hearted, you know."

"It is a great blow to me—a great blow."

Claudia looked as if she would like to say "Fudge!" but restrained herself and, with the daring characteristic of her, placed her hand on his arm.

"I am so sorry, Mr. Haddington. How it must gall you to see their happiness! I can understand you turning to me as if in self-protection. But you should not ask a lady to marry you because you're piqued with another lady. It isn't kind; it isn't, indeed."

Haddington was a little at loss.

"Indeed, you're wholly wrong. Lady Claudia. Indeed, if you come to that, I don't see that they are particularly rapturous."

"You don't mean you think they're unhappy? Mr. Haddington, I am so grieved!"

"Do you mean to say you don't agree with me?"

"You mustn't ask me. But, oh! I'm so sorry you think so too. Isn't it strange? So suited to one another—she so beautiful, he so clever, and both rich!"

"Miss Bernard is hardly rich, is she?"

"Not as Mr. Lane is, of course. She seems rich to me—forty thousand pounds, I think. Ah, Mr. Haddington, if only you had met her sooner!"

"I shouldn't have had much chance against Lane."

"Why do you say that? If you only knew—"

"What?"

"I mustn't tell you. How sad that it's too late!"

"Is it?"

"Of course. They're *engaged*!"

"An engagement isn't a marriage. If I thought—"

"Yes?"

"But I can't think of that now. Good-by, Claudia. We may not meet again."

"Oh, you won't go away? You mustn't let me drive you away. Oh, please, Mr. Haddington! Think, if you go, it must all come out! I should be so very, very distressed."

"If you ask me, I will try to stay."

"Yes, yes, stay—but forget all this. And never think again of the other—about them, I mean. You will stay?"

"Yes, I will stay," said Haddington.

"Unless it makes you too unhappy to see Eugene's triumph in Kate's love?"

"I don't believe much in that. If that's the only thing—but I must go. I see your brother coming up the hill."

"Yes, go; and I'll never tell that you tried me as—as a second string!"

"That's very unjust!" he protested, but more weakly.

"No, it isn't. I know your heart, and I do pity you."

"Perhaps I shall not ask for pity, Lady Claudia!"

"Oh, you mustn't think of that!"

"It was you who put it in my head."

"Oh, what have I done!"

Haddington smiled, and with a last squeeze of her hand turned and walked away.

Claudia put her handkerchief into her pocket and went to meet her brother.

Haddington returned alone to the house. Although suffering under a natural feeling of annoyance at discovering that he was not foremost in Claudia's heart, as he had led himself to suppose, he was yet keenly alive to the fact that the interview had its consolatory aspect. In the first place, there is a fiction that a lady who respects herself does not fall in love with a man whom she suspects to be in love with somebody else; and Haddington's mind, though of no mean order in some ways, was not of a sort to rise above fictions. He comforted his vanity with the thought that Claudia had, by a conscious effort, checked a nascent affection for him, which, if allowed unimpeded growth, would have developed into a passion. Again, that astute young lady had very accurately conjectured his state of mind, while her pledge of secrecy disposed of the difficulty in the way of a too rapid transfer of his attentions. If Claudia did not complain, nay, counseled such action, who had a right to object? It was true she had eagerly disclaimed any intention of inciting him to try to break the ties that now bound Miss Bernard. But, he reflected, the important point was not the view she took of the morality of such an attempt, on which her authority was nought, but her opinion of its chances of success, which was obviously not wholly unfavorable. He did not trouble himself to inquire closely into any personal motive she may have had. It was enough for him that she, a person likely to be well informed, had allowed him to see that, to her thinking, the relations between the engaged pair were of a character to inspire in the mind of another aspirant hope rather than despair.

Having reached this conclusion, Haddington recognized that his first step must be to put Miss Bernard in touch with the position of affairs. It may seem a delicate matter to hint to your host's *fiancée* that if she, on mature reflection, likes you better than him, there is still time; but Haddington was not afflicted with delicacy. After all, in such a case a great deal depends upon the lady, and Haddington, though doubtful how Kate would regard a direct proposal to break off her engagement, was yet tolerably confident that she would not betray him to Eugene.

He found her seated on the terrace that was the usual haunt of the ladies in the forenoon and the scene of Eugene's dutiful labors as reader-aloud. Kate was not looking amiable; and scarce six feet from her there lay open on the ground a copy of the Laureate's works.

"I hope I'm not disturbing you, Miss Bernard?"

"Oh, no. You see, I am alone. Mr. Lane was here just now, but he's gone."

"How's that?" asked Haddington, seating himself.

"He got a telegram, read it, flung his book away, and rushed off."

"Did he say what it was about?"

"No; I didn't ask him."

A pause ensued. It was a little difficult to make a start.

"And so you are alone?"

"Yes, as you see."

"I am alone too. Shall we console one another?"

"I don't want consolation, thanks," said Kate, a little ungraciously. "But," she added more kindly, "you know I'm always glad of your company."

"I wish I could think so."

"Why don't you think so?"

"Well, Miss Bernard, engaged people are generally rather indifferent to the rest of the world.

"Even to telegrams?"

"Ah! poor Lane!"

"I don't think Mr. Lane is in much need of pity."

"No—rather of envy."

Kate did not look displeased.

"Still, a man is to be pitied if he does not appreciate—"

"Mr. Haddington!"

"I beg your pardon. I ought not to have said that. But it is hard—there, I am offending you again!"

"Yes, you must not talk like that. It's wrong; it would be wrong even if you meant it."

"Do you think I don't mean it?"

"That would be very discreditable—but not so bad."

"You know I mean it," he said, in a low voice. "God knows I would have said nothing if—"

"If what?"

"I shall offend you more than ever. But how can I stand by and see *that*?" and Haddington pointed with fine scorn to the neglected book.

Kate was not agitated. She seldom was. In a tone of grave rebuke, she said:

"You must never speak like this again. I thought I saw something of it. ["Good!" thought Haddington.] But whatever may be my lot, I am now bound to it. Pledges are not to be broken."

"Are they not being virtually broken?" he asked, growing bolder as he saw she listened to him.

Kate rose.

"You are not angry?"

"I cannot be angry if it is as you say. But please understand I cannot listen. It is not honorable. No—don't say anything else. But you must go away."

Haddington made no further effort to step her. He was well content. When a lady hears you hint that her betrothed is less devoted than you would be in his place, and merely says the giving of such a hint is wrong, it may be taken that her sole objection to it is on the score of morality; and it is to be feared that objections based on this ground are not the most efficacious in checking forward lovers. Perhaps Miss Bernard thought they were. Haddington didn't believe she did.

"Go away?" he said to himself. "Hardly! The play is just beginning. Little Lady Claudia wasn't far out."

It is very possible she was not far out in her estimation of Mr. Haddington's character, as well as in her forecast of his prospects. But the fruits of her shrewdness on this point were happily hid from the gentleman concerned.

CHAPTER IV.

Sir Roderick Ayre Inspects Mr. Morewood's Masterpiece.

About a fortnight later than the last recorded incident two men were smoking on the lawn at Millstead Manor. One was Morewood; the other had arrived only the day before and was the Sir Roderick Ayre to whom reference has been made.

"Upon my word, Morewood," said Sir Roderick, as the painter sat down by him, "one can't go anywhere without meeting you!"

"That's since you took to intellectual company," said Morewood, grinning.

"I haven't taken to intellectual company," said Sir Roderick, with languid indignation.

"In the general upheaval, intellectual company has risen in the scale."

"And so has at last come up to your pinnacle?"

"And so has reached me, where I have been for centuries."

"A sort of perpetual dove on Ararat?"

"My dear Morewood, I am told you know everything except the Bible. Why choose your allusions from the one unfamiliar source?"

"And how do you like your new neighbor?"

"What new neighbor?"

"Intellect."

"Oh! well, as personified in you it's a not unwholesome astringent. But we may take an overdose."

"Depends on the capacity of the constitution, of course," said Morewood.

"One objectionable quality it has," pursued Sir Roderick, apparently unheedful.

"Yes?"

"A disposition toward what boys call 'scoring.' That will, no doubt, be eradicated as it rises more in society. *Apropos*, what are you doing down here?"

"As an artist, I study your insolence professionally, Ayre, and it doesn't annoy me. I came down here to do nothing. I have stayed to paint Stafford."

"Ah! is Stafford then a professional saint?"

"He's an uncommon fine fellow. You're not fit to black his boots."

"I am not fit to black anybody's boots," responded Sir Roderick. "It's the other way. What's he doing down here?"

"I don't know. Says he's writing a book. Do you know Lady Claudia well?"

"Yes. Known her since she was a child."

"She seems uncommonly appreciative."

"Of Stafford?"

"Yes."

"Oh, well! it's her way. It always has been the way of the Territons. They only began, you know, about three hundred years ago, and ever since—"

"Oh, I don't want their history—a lot of scoundrels, no doubt, like all your old families. Only—I say, Ayre, I should like to show you a head of Stafford I've done."

"I won't buy it!" said Sir Roderick, with affected trepidation.

"You be damned!" said Morewood. "But I should like to hear what you think of it."

"What do he and the rest of them think?"

"I haven't shown it to any one."

"Why not?"

"Wait till you've seen it."

"I should think Stafford would make rather a good head. He's got just that—"

"Hush! Here he comes!"

As he spoke, Stafford and Claudia came up the drive and emerged on to the lawn. They did not see the others and appeared to be deep in conversation. Stafford was talking vehemently and Claudia listening with a look of amused mutiny on her face.

"He's sworn off, hasn't he?" asked Ayre.

"Yes."

"She doesn't care for him?"

"I don't think so; but a man can't tell."

"Nonsense!" said Ayre. "What's Eugene up to?"

"Oh, you know he's booked."

"Kate Bernard?"

"Yes."

"Tell you what, Morewood, I'll lay you—"

"No, you won't. Come and see the picture. It's the finest thing—in its way—I ever did."

"Going to exhibit it?"

"I'm going to work up and exhibit another I've done of him, not this one; at least, I'm afraid he won't stand this one."

"Gad! Have you painted him with horns and a tail?"

Whereto Morewood answered only:

"Come and see."

As they went in, they met Eugene, hands in pockets and pipe in mouth, looking immensely bored.

"Dr. Livingstone, I presume?" said he. "Excuse the mode of address, but I've not seen a soul all the morning, and thought I must have dropped down somewhere in Africa. It's monstrous! I ask about ten people to my house, and I never have a soul to speak to!"

"Where's Miss Bernard?" asked Ayre.

"Kate is learning constitutional principles from Haddington in the shrubbery. Lady Claudia is learning sacerdotal principles from Stafford in the shrubbery. My mother is learning equine principles from Bob Territon in the stables. You are learning immoral principles from Morewood on the lawn. I don't complain, but is there anything a man can do?"

"Yes, there's a picture to be seen—Morewood's latest."

"Good!"

"I don't know that I shall show it to Lane."

"Oh, get out!" said Eugene. "I shall summon the servants to my aid. Who's it of?"

"Stafford," said Ayre.

"The Pope in full canonicals?"

"All right, Lane. But you're a friend of his, and you mayn't like it."

They entered the billiard-room, a long building that ran out from the west wing of the house. In the extreme end of it Morewood had extemporized a studio, attracted by the good light.

"Give me a good top-light," he had said, "and I wouldn't change places with an arch-angel!"

"Your lights, top or otherwise, are not such," Eugene remarked, "as to make it likely the berth will be offered you."

"This picture is, I understand, Eugene, a stunner. Give us chairs and some brandy and soda and trot it out," said Ayre.

Morewood was unmoved by their frivolity. He tugged at his ragged red beard for a moment or two while they were settling themselves.

"I'll show you this first," he said, taking up one of the canvases that leant against the wall.

It was a beautiful sketch of a half-length figure, and represented Stafford in the garb of a monk, gazing up with eager eyes, full of the vision of the Eternal City beyond the skies. It was the face of a devotee and a visionary, and yet it was full of strength and resolution; and there was in it the look of a man who had put aside all except the service and the contemplation of the Divine.

Ayre forgot to sneer, and Eugene murmured:

"Glorious! What a subject! And, old fellow, what an artist!"

"That is good," said Morewood quietly. "It's fine, but as a matter of painting the other is still better. I caught him looking like that one morning. He came out before breakfast, very early, into the garden. I was out there, but he didn't see me, and he stood looking up like that for ever so long, his lips just parted and his eyes straining through the veil, as you see that. It may be all nonsense, but—fine, isn't it?"

The two men nodded.

"Now for the other," said Ayre. "By Jove! I feel as if I'd been in church."

"The other I got only three or four days ago. Again I was a Paul Pry,—we have to be, you know, if we're to do anything worth doing,—and I took him while he sat. But I dare say you'd better see it first."

He took another and smaller picture and placed it on the easel, standing for a moment between it and the onlookers and studying it closely. Then he stepped aside in silence.

It was merely a head—nothing more—standing out boldly from a dark background. The face was again Stafford's, but the presentment differed strangely. It was still beautiful; it had even a beauty the other had not, the beauty of youth and passion. The devotee was gone; in his place was a face that, in spite of the ascetic cast of feature, was so lighted up with the fire of love and longing that it might have stood for a Leander or a Romeo. It expressed an eager yearning, that made it seem to be craning out of the picture in the effort to reach that unknown object on which the eyes were fixed with such devouring passion.

The men sat looking at it in amazement. Eugene was half angry, half alarmed. Ayre was closely studying the picture, his old look of cynical amusement struggling with a surprise which it was against his profession to admit. They forgot to praise the picture; but Morewood was well content with their tacit homage.

"The finest thing I ever did—on my life; one of the finest things any one ever did," he murmured; "and I can't show it!"

"No," said Eugene.

Ayre rose and took his stand before the picture. Then he got a chair, choosing the lowest he could find, and sat down, sitting well back. This attitude brought him exactly under the gaze of the eyes.

"Is it your diabolic fancy," he said, "or did you honestly copy it?"

"I never struck closer to what I saw," the painter replied. "It's not my doing; he looked like that."

"Then who was sitting, as it were, where I am now?"

"Yes," said Morewood. "I thought you couldn't miss it."

"Who was it?" asked Eugene, in an excited way.

The others looked keenly at him for a moment.

"You know," said Morewood. "Claudia Territon. She was sitting there reading. He had a book, too, but had laid it down on his knee. She sat reading, and he looking. In a moment I caught the look. Then she put down the book; and as she turned to him to speak, in a second it was gone, and he was not this picture nor the other, but as we know him every day."

"She didn't see?" asked Eugene.

"No."

"Thank God!" he cried. Then in a moment, recollecting himself, he looked at the two men, and saw what he had done. They tried to look as if they noticed nothing.

"You must destroy that thing, Morewood," said he.

Morewood's face was a study.

"I would as soon," he said deliberately, "cut off my right hand."

"I'll give you a thousand pounds for it," said Eugene.

"What would you do with it?"

"Burn it."

"Then you shouldn't have it for ten thousand."

"I thought you'd say that. But he mustn't see it."

"Why, Lane, you're as bad as a child. It's a man in love, that's all."

"If he saw it," said Eugene, "he'd hang himself."

"Oh, gently!" said Ayre. "If you ask me, I expect Stafford will pretty soon get beyond any surprise at the revelation. He must walk his path, like all of us. It can't matter to you, you know," he added, with a sharp glance.

"No, it can't matter to me," said Eugene steadily.

"Put it away, Morewood, and come out of doors. Perhaps you'd better not leave it about, at present at any rate."

Morewood took down the picture and placed it in a large portfolio, which he locked, and accompanied Ayre. Eugene made no motion to come with them, and they left him sitting there.

"The atmosphere," said Sir Roderick, looking up into the clear summer sky, "is getting thundery and complicated. I hate complications! They're a bore! I think I shall go."

"I shan't. It will be interesting."

"Perhaps you're right. I'll stay a little while."

"Ah! here you are. I've been looking for somebody to amuse me."

The speaker was Claudia, looking very fresh and cool in her soft white dress.

"What have you done with the Pope?" asked Ayre.

"He gave me to understand he had wasted enough time on me, and went in to write."

"I should think he was right," said Sir Roderick.

"I dare say," said Claudia carelessly.

Her conscience was evidently quite at ease; but they did not know whether this meant that her actions had deserved no blame. However, they were neither of them men to judge such a case as hers harshly.

"If I were fifteen years younger," said Ayre, "I would waste all my time on you."

"Why, you're only about forty," said Claudia. "That's not too old."

"Good!" said he, smiling. "Life in the old dog yet, eh? But go in and see Lane. He's in the billiard-room, thinking over his sins and getting low-spirited."

"And I shall be a change?"

"I don't know about that. Perhaps he's a homoeopathist."

"I hate you!" said Claudia, with a very kind glance, as she pursued her way in the direction indicated.

"She means no harm," said Morewood.

"But she may do the devil of a lot. We can't help it, can we?"

"No—not our business if we could," said Morewood.

Claudia paused for a moment at the door. Eugene was still sitting with his head on his hand.

"It's very odd," thought she. "What's he looking at the easel for? There's nothing on it!"

Then she began to sing. Eugene looked up.

"Is it you, Lady Claudia?"

"Yes. Why are you moping here?"

"Where's Stafford?"

"Everybody," said Claudia impatiently, throwing her hat, and herself after it, on a lounge, "asks me where Father Stafford is. I don't know, Mr. Lane; and what's more, at this moment I don't care. Have you nothing better than that to say to me when I come to look for you?"

Eugene pulled himself together. Tragedy airs would be insufferable.

"True, most beauteous damsel!" he said. "I am remiss. For the purposes of the moment, hang Stafford! What shall we do?"

She got up and came close to him.

"Mr. Lane," she whispered, "what do you think there is in the stable?"

"I know what there isn't: that's a horse fit to ride."

"A libel! a libel! But there is [in a still lower whisper] a *sociable*."

"A what?"

"A sociable."

"Do you mean a tricycle?"

"Yes—for two."

"Oho!" said Eugene, gently chuckling.

"Wouldn't it be fun?"

"On the road?"

"N—no, perhaps not; round the park."

"Hush! S'death! if Kate saw us! Where is she?"

"I saw her last with Mr. Haddington."

"In the scheme of creation everything has its use," replied Eugene tranquilly. "Haddington supplies a felt want."

"Be quiet. But will you?"

"Yes; come along. Be swift and silent."

"I must go and put on an old frock."

"All right; be quick."

"What is the use?" Eugene pondered; "I can't have her, and Stafford may as well—if he will. Will he, I wonder? And would she? Oh, Lord! what a nuisance they are! By Jove! I should like to see Kate's face if she spots us."

A few minutes later the strange and unedifying sight of Lady Claudia Territon and Mr. Lane, mounted on a very rickety old "sociable," presented itself to the gaping gaze of several laborers in the park. Claudia was in her most boisterous spirits; Eugene, by one of the quick transitions of his nature, was hardly less elate. Up-hill they toiled and down-hill they raced, getting, as the manner of "cyclists" is, very warm and rather oily. But retribution lagged not. Down a steep hill they came, round a sharp turn they went, and, alas, over into a ditch they fell. This was bad enough, but in the calm seclusion of a garden seat, perched on a knoll just above them, the sinners, as they rose, dirty but unhurt, beheld Miss Bernard! For a moment all was consternation. What would she say?

It was a curious thing, but Kate seemed as embarrassed as themselves, and she said nothing except:

"Oh, I hope you're not hurt!" and said this in a hasty way and with ostentatious amiability.

Eugene was surprised. But as his eyes wandered, they fell on Haddington, and that rising politician held awkwardly in his hand, and was trying to convey behind his back, what looked very like a lady's glove. Now Miss Bernard had only one glove on.

"The battery is spiked," he whispered triumphantly. "Come along, Lady Claudia."

Claudia hadn't seen what Eugene had, but she obeyed, and off they went again, airily waving their hands.

"What's the matter with her?" she asked.

Eugene was struggling with laughter.

"Didn't you see? Haddington had her glove! Splendid!"

Claudia, regardless of safety, turned for an instant, a flushed, smiling face to him. He was about to speak, but she turned away again, exclaiming:

"Quick! I've promised to meet Father Stafford at twelve, and I mustn't keep him waiting. I wouldn't miss it for the world!"

Eugene was checked; Claudia saw it. What she thought is not revealed, but they returned home in somewhat gloomy silence. And it is a comfort to the narrator, and it is to be hoped to the reader, to think that Mr. Eugene Lane got something besides pleasure out of his discreditable performance and his lamentable want of proper feeling.

CHAPTER V.

How Three Gentlemen Acted for the Best.

The schemers schemed and the waiters upon events waited with considerable patience, but although the days wore on, the situation showed little signs of speedy development. Matters were in fact in a rather puzzling position. The friendship and intimacy between Claudia and Stafford continued to increase. Eugene, whether in penitence or in pique, had turned with renewed zeal to his proper duties, and was no longer content to allow Kate to be monopolized by Haddington. The latter's attentions had indeed been in danger of becoming too marked, and it is, perhaps, not uncharitable to attribute Kate's apparent avoidance of them as much to considerations of expediency as of principle. At the same time, there was no coolness between Eugene and Haddington, and when his guest presented a valid excuse and proposed departure, Eugene met the suggestion with an obviously sincere opposition. Sir Roderick really could not make out what was going on. Now Sir Roderick disliked being puzzled; it conveyed a reflection on his acuteness, and he therefore was a sharer in the perturbation of mind that evidently afflicted some of his companions, in spite of their decorous behavior. But contentment was not wanting in some hearts. Morewood was happy in the pursuit of his art and in arguments with Stafford; and Bob Territon had found refuge in an energetic attempt to organize and train a Manor team to do battle with the village cricket club, headed as it had been for thirty years past by the Rector. Moreover, Stafford himself still seemed tranquil. It would have been difficult for most men to fail to understand their true position in such a case more fully than he, in spite of his usual penetration of vision, had succeeded in doing. But he was now in a strange country, and the landmarks of feeling whereby the experienced traveler on such paths can learn and note, even if he cannot check, his descent, were to Stafford unmeaning and empty of warning. Of course, he knew he liked Claudia's society; he found her talk at once a change, a rest, and a stimulus; he had even become aware that of all the people at the Manor, except his old friend and host, she had for him the most interest and attraction; perhaps he had even suffered at times that sense of vacancy of all the chairs when her chair was vacant that should have told him of his state if anything would. But he did not see; he was blind in this matter, even as, say, Ayre or Morewood would have proved blind if called upon to study and describe the mental process of a religious conversation. He was yet far from realizing that an influence had entered his life in force strong enough to contend with that which had so long ruled him with undivided sway. It was the part of a friend to hope and try that he might go with his own heart yet a secret to him. So hoped Eugene. But Eugene, unnerved by self-suspicion, would not lift a finger to hasten his friend's departure, lest he should seem to himself, or be without perceiving it even himself, alert to save his friend, only because his friend's salvation would be to his own comfort.

Sir Roderick Ayre, however, was not restrained by Eugene's scruples nor inspired by Eugene's devotion to Stafford. Stafford interested him, but he was not his friend, and Ayre did not understand, or, if truth be told, appreciate the almost reverential attitude which Eugene, usually so very devoid of reverence, adopted toward him. Ayre thought Stafford's vow nonsense, and that if he was in love with Claudia Territon there was no harm done.

"Many people have been," he said, "and many will be, before the little witch grows old and—no, by Jove! she'll never grow ugly!"

Trivial as the matter seemed, looked at in this light, it had yet enough of human interest about it to decide him to leave the grouse alone, and wait patiently for the partridges at Millstead. After all, he had shot grouse and most other things for thirty years; and, as he said, "The parson was a change, and the house deuced comfortable, and old Eugene a good fellow."

Now it came to pass one day that the devil, having a spare hour on his hands, and remembering that he had often met with a hospitable reception from Sir Roderick, to say nothing of having a bowing acquaintance with Morewood, looked in at the Manor, and finding his old quarters at Sir Roderick's swept and garnished, incontinently took up his abode there, and proceeded to look round for some suitable occupation. When this momentous but invisible event accomplished itself, Sir Roderick was outwardly engaged in the innocent and aimless pursuit of knocking the billiard balls about and listening absently to a discourse from Morewood on the essential truths which he (Morewood) had grasped and presented alone of modern artists. The theme was not exhilarating, and Sir Roderick's tenant soon grew very tired of it; the presentment of truth, indeed, essential or otherwise, not being a matter that concerned him. But in the course of an inspection of Sir Roderick's consciousness, he had come across something that appeared worth following up, and toward it he proceeded to direct his entertainer's conversation.

"I say, Morewood," said Ayre, breaking in on the discourse, "do you think it's fair to keep that fellow Stafford in the dark?"

"Is he in the dark?"

"It's a queer thing, but he is. I never knew a man who was in love before without knowing it,—they say women are that way,—but then I never met a 'Father' before."

"What do you propose, since you insist on gossiping?"

"It isn't gossip; it's Christian feeling. Some one ought to tell the poor beggar."

"Perhaps you'd like to."

"I should, but it would seem like a liberty, and I never take liberties. You do constantly, so you might as well take this one."

"I like that! Why, the man's a stranger! If he ought to be told at all, Lane's the man to do it."

"Yes, but you see, Lane—"

"That's quite true; I forgot. But isn't he better left alone to get over it?"

Sir Roderick, unprejudiced, might have conceded the point. But the prompter intervened.

"What I'm thinking about is this: is it fair to her? I don't say she's in love with him, but she admires him immensely. They're always together, and—well, it's plain what's likely enough to happen. If it does, what will be said? Who'll believe he did it unconsciously? And if he breaks her heart, how is it better because he did it unconsciously?"

"You are unusually benevolent," said Morewood dryly.

"Hang it! a man has some feelings."

"You're a humbug, Ayre!"

"Never mind what I am. You won't tell him?"

"No."

"It would be a very interesting problem."

"It would."

"That vow of his is all nonsense, ain't it?"

"Utter nonsense!"

"Why shouldn't he have his chance of being happy in a reasonable way? I shouldn't wonder if she took him."

"No more should I."

"Upon my soul, I believe it's a duty! I say, Morewood, do you think he'd see it for himself from the picture?"

"Of course he would. No one could help it."

"Will you let him see it?"

Morewood took a turn or two up and down, tugging his beard. The issue was doubtful. A certain auditor of the conversation, perceiving this, hastily transferred himself from one interlocutor to the other.

"I'll tell you what I'll do: I'll let him see it if Lane agrees. I'll leave it to Lane."

48

"Rather rough on Lane, isn't it?"

"A little strong emotion of any kind won't do Lane any harm."

"Perhaps not. We will train our young friend's mind to cope with moral problems. He'll never get on in the world nowadays unless he can do that. It's now part of a gentleman's—still more of a lady's—education."

Eugene was clearly wanted. By some agency, into which it is needless to inquire, though we may have suspicions, at that moment Eugene strolled into the billiard-room.

"We have a little question to submit to you, my dear fellow," said Ayre blandly.

Eugene looked at him suspiciously. He had been a good deal worried the last few days, and had a dim idea that he deserved it, which deprived him of the sense of unmerited suffering—a most valuable consolation in time of trouble.

"It's about Stafford. You remember the head of him Morewood did, and the conclusion we drew from it—or, rather, it forced upon us?"

Eugene nodded, instinctively assuming his most nonchalant air.

"We think he's a bad case. What think you?"

"I agree—at least, I suppose I do. I haven't thought much about it."

Ayre thought the indifference overdone, but he took no notice of it.

"We are inclined to think he ought to be shown that picture. I am clear about it; Morewood doubts. And we are going to refer it to you."

"You'd better leave me out."

"Not at all. You're a friend of his, known him all your life, and you'll know best what will be for his good."

"If you insist on asking me, I think you had better let it alone."

"Wait a minute. Why do you say that?"

"Because it will be a shock to him."

"No doubt, at first. He's got some silly notion in his head about not marrying, and about its being sinful to fall in love, and all, that."

"It won't make him happier to be refused."

Ayre leant forward in his chair, and said: "How do you know she'll refuse him?"

"I don't know. How should I know?"

"Do you think it likely?"

"Is that a fair question?" asked Morewood.

"Perfectly," said Eugene, with an expressionless face. "But it's one I have no means of answering."

"He's plucky," thought Ayre. "Would you give the same answer you gave just now if you thought she'd take him?"

It was certainly hard on Eugene. Was he bound, against even a tolerably strong feeling of his own, to give Stafford every chance? It is not fair to a man to make him a judge where he is in truth a party. Ayre had no mercy for him.

"For the sake of a trumpery pledge is he to throw away his own happiness—and mark you, Lane, perhaps hers?"

Eugene did not wince.

"If there's a chance of success, he ought to be given the opportunity of exercising his own judgment," he said quietly. "It would distress him immensely, but we should have no right to keep it from him. And I suppose there's always a chance of success."

"Go and get the picture, Morewood," said Sir Roderick. Then, when the painter was looking in the portfolio, he said abruptly to Eugene:

"You could say nothing else."

"No. That's why you asked me, I suppose. I hope I'm an interesting subject. You dig pretty deep."

"Serves you right!" said Ayre composedly. "Why were you ever such an ass?"

"God knows!" groaned Eugene.

Morewood returned.

"He's due here in ten minutes to sit to me. Are you going to stay?"

"No. You be doing something else, and let that thing stand on the easel."

"Pleasant for me, isn't it?" asked Morewood.

"Are you ashamed of yourself for snatching it?"

"Not a bit."

"All right, then; what's the matter? Come along, Eugene. After all, you know you'll like showing it. For an outsider, like yourself, it's really a deuced clever little bit. Perhaps they will make you an Associate if Stafford will let you show it."

Morewood ignored the taunt, and sat down by the window on pretense of touching up a sketch. He had not been there long when he heard Stafford come in, and became conscious that he had caught sight of the picture. He did not look up, and heard no sound. A long pause followed. Then he felt a strong grip on his shoulder, and Stafford whispered:

"It is my face?"

"You see it is."

"You did it?"

"Yes. I ought to beg your pardon," and he looked up. Stafford was pale as death, and trembling.

"When?"

"A few days ago."

"On your oath—no, you don't believe that—on your honor, is it truth?"

"Yes, it is."

"You saw it—just as it is there?"

"Yes, it is exact. I had no right to take it or to show it you."

"What does that matter, man? Do you think I care about that? But—yes, it is true. God help me!"

"We have seen it, you know. It was time you saw it."

"Time, indeed!"

"Where's the harm?" asked Morewood, in a rough effort at comfort.

"The harm? But you don't understand. It is the face of a beast!"

"My dear fellow, that's stuff! It's only the face of a lover."

Stafford looked at him in a dazed way.

"I wish you'd let me go back to my room, Morewood, and give me that picture. No—I won't hurt it."

"Take it, then, and pull yourself together. What's the harm, again I say? And if she loves you—"

"What?" he cried eagerly. Then, checking himself, "Hold your peace, in Heaven's name, and let me go!"

He went his way, and Morewood leaped from the window to find the other two. He found them, but not alone. Ayre was discoursing to Claudia and appeared entirely oblivious of the occurrence which he had precipitated. Eugene was walking up and down with Kate Bernard. It is necessary to listen to what the latter couple were saying.

"This is sad news, Kate," Eugene said. "Why are you going to leave us?"

"My aunt wants me to go with her to Buxton in September, and we're going to have a few days on the river before that."

"Then we shall not meet again for some time?"

"No. Of course I shall write to you."

"Thank you—I hope you will. You've had a pleasant time, I hope? Who are to be your river party?"

"Oh, just ourselves and one or two girls and men. Lord Rickmansworth is to be there a day or two, if he can. And—oh, yes, Mr. Haddington, I think."

"Isn't Haddington staying here?"

"I don't know. I understood not. So your party will break up," Kate went on. "Of course, Claudia can't stay when I go."

"Why not?"

"Really, Eugene, it would be hardly the thing."

"I believe my mother is not thinking of going."

"Do you mean you will ask Claudia?"

"I certainly cannot ask her to curtail her visit."

"Anyhow, Father Stafford goes soon, and she won't stay then."

This last shaft accomplished Miss Bernard's presumable object. Eugene lost his temper.

"Forgive me for saying so, Kate," he said, "but really at times your mind seems to me positively vulgar."

"I am not going to quarrel. I am quite aware of what you want."

"What's that?"

"An opportunity for quarreling."

"If that's all, I might have found several. But come, Kate, it's no use, and not very dignified, to squabble. We haven't got on so well as we might. But I dare say it's my fault."

"Do you want to throw me over?" asked Kate scornfully.

"For Heaven's sake, don't talk like a breach-of-promise plaintiff! I am and always have been perfectly ready to fulfill my engagement. But you don't make it easy for me. Unless you 'throw me over,' as you are pleased to phrase it, things will remain as they are."

"I have been taught to consider an engagement as binding as a marriage."

"No warrant for such a view in Holy Scripture."

"And whatever my feelings may be—and you can hardly wonder if, after your conduct, they are not what they were—I shall consider myself bound."

"I have never proposed anything else."

"Your conduct with Claudia—"

"I must ask you to leave Lady Claudia alone. If you come to that—but there, I was just going to scratch back like a school-girl. Let us remember our manners, if nothing else."

"And our principles," added Kate haughtily.

"By all means, and forget our deviations from them. And now this conversation may as well end, may it not?"

Kate's only answer was to walk straight away to the house.

Eugene joined Claudia; Ayre, in his absence, had been reinforced by the accession of Bob Territon.

"Kate's going to-morrow," Eugene announced.

"So I heard," said Claudia. "We must go, too—we have been here a terrible time."

"Why?"

"It's all nonsense!" interposed Bob decisively; "we can't go for a week. The match is fixed for next Wednesday."

"But," said Claudia, "I'm not going to play."

"I am," said Bob. "And where do you propose to go to?"

"No, Lady Claudia," said Eugene, "you must see us through the great day. I really wish you would. The whole county's coming, and it will be too much for my mother alone. After the cricket-match, if you still insist, the deluge!"

"I'll ask Mrs. Lane. She'll tell me what to do."

"Good child!" said Sir Roderick. "I am going to stay right away till the birds. And as Lane says I ain't to have any birds unless I field at long-leg, I am going to field at long-leg."

"Splendid!" cried Claudia, clapping her hands; "Sir Roderick Ayre at a rustic cricket-match! Mr. Morewood shall sketch you."

"I've had enough of sketching just now," said Morewood. Ayre and Eugene looked up. Morewood nodded slightly.

"Where's Stafford?" asked Ayre.

"In his room—at work, I suppose. He put off my sitting."

"Never mind Father Stafford," said Claudia decisively. "Who is going to play tennis? I shall play with Sir Roderick."

"I'd much rather sit still in the shade," pleaded Sir Roderick.

"You're a very rude *old* gentleman! But you must play, all the same—against Bob and Mr. Morewood."

"Where do I come in?" asked Eugene. "Mayn't I do anything, Lady Claudia?"

The others were looking after the net and the racquets, and Claudia was left with him for a moment.

"Yes," she said; "you may go and sit on Kate's trunks till they lock."

"Wait a little while; I will be revenged on you. I want, though, to ask you a question."

"Oh! Is it a question that no one else—say Kate, for instance—could help you with?"

"It's not about myself."

"Is it about me?"

"Yes."

"What's the matter, Mr. Lane? Is it anything serious?"

"Very."

"Nonsense!" said Claudia. "You really mustn't do it, Mr. Lane, or I can't stay for the cricket-match."

"We shall be desolate. Stafford's going in a few days."

But Claudia's face was entirely guileless as she replied:

"Is he? I'm so sorry! But he's looking much stronger, isn't he?"

With which she departed to join Sir Roderick, who had been spending the interval in extracting from Morewood an account of Stafford's behavior.

"Hard hit, was he?" he concluded.

"He looked it."

"Wonder what he'll do! I'll give you five to four he asks her."

"Done!" said Morewood; "in fives."

CHAPTER VI.

Father Stafford Keeps Vigil.

Dinner that evening at the Manor was not a very brilliant affair. Stafford did not appear, pleading that it was a Friday, and a strict fast for him. Kate was distinctly out of temper, and treated the company in general, and Eugene in particular, with frigidity. Everybody felt that the situation was somewhat strained, and in consequence the pleasant flow of personal talk that marks parties of friends was dried up at its source. The discussion of general topics was found to be a relief.

"The utter uselessness of such a class as Ayre represents," said Morewood emphatically, taking up a conversation that had started no one quite knew how, "must strike every sensible man."

"At least they buy pictures," said Eugene.

"On the contrary, they now sell old masters, and empty the pockets of would-be buyers."

"They are very ornamental," remarked Claudia.

"In some cases, undoubtedly," said Morewood.

"If you mean a titled class," said Ayre, "I quite agree. I object to titles. They only confuse ranks. A sweep is made a lord, and outsiders think he's a gentlemen."

"Come, you're a baronet yourself, you know," said Eugene.

"It's true," admitted Ayre, with a sigh; "but it happened a long while ago, and we've nearly lived it down."

"Take care they don't make you a peer!"

"I have passed a busy life in avoiding it. After all, there's a chance. I'm not a brewer or a lawyer, or anything of that kind. But still, the fear of it has paralyzed my energies and compelled me to squander my fortune. They don't make poor men peers."

"That ought to have been allowed to weigh in the balance in favor of Dives," suggested Eugene.

"Not a bit," said Ayre. "Depend upon it, they kept it for him down below."

"I hate cynicism!" said Claudia, suddenly and aggressively.

Ayre put up his eyeglass.

"*Après?*"

"It's all affectation."

"Really, Lady Claudia, you might be quite old, from the way you talk. That is one of the illusions of age, which, by the way, have not received enough attention."

"That's very true," said Eugene. "Old people think the world better than it is because their faculties don't enable them to make such demands upon it."

"My dear Eugene," said Mrs. Lane pertinently, "what can you know about it? As we grow old we grow charitable."

"And why is that?" asked Morewood; "not because you think better of other people, but because you know more of yourself."

"That is so," said Ayre. "Standing midway between youth and age, I am an arbiter. You judge others by yourself. In youth you have an unduly good opinion of yourself, that unduly depresses your opinion of others. In age it's the opposite way. But who knows which is more wrong?"

"At least let us hope age is right, Sir Roderick," said Mrs. Lane.

"By all means," said he.

"All this doesn't touch my point," said Claudia. "You are accounting for it as if it existed. My point was that it didn't exist. I said it was all affectation."

"And not the only sort of affectation of the same kind!" said Kate Bernard, with remarkable emphasis.

Sir Roderick enjoyed a troubled sea. Turning to Kate, with a rapid side glance at Claudia on the way, he said:

"That's interesting. How do you mean, Miss Bernard?"

"All attempts to put one's self forward, to be peculiar, and so on, are the same kind of affectation, and are odious—especially in women."

There was nothing very much in the words, and Kate was careful to look straight in front of her as she uttered them. Still they told.

"You mean," said Ayre, "there may be an affectation of freshness and enthusiasm—gush, in fact—as bad, or worse, than cynicism, and really springing from the same root?"

Kate had not arrived at any such definite meaning, but she nodded her head.

"An assumed sprightliness," continued Ayre cheerfully, "perhaps coquettishness?"

"Exactly," Kate assented, "and a way of pushing into conversations which my mother used to say girls had better let alone."

This was tolerably direct, but it did not satisfy Ayre's malicious humor, and he was on the point of a new question when Haddington, who had taken no part in the previous conversation, but had his reasons for interfering now, put in suavely:

"If Miss Bernard and you, Ayre, will forgive me, are we not wandering from the point?"

"Was there any point to wander from?" suggested Eugene.

So they drifted through the evening, skirting the coast of quarrels and talking of everything except that of which they were thinking. Verily, love affairs do not always conduce to social enjoyment— more especially other people's love affairs. Still, Sir Roderick Ayre was entertained.

Meanwhile, Stafford sat in his room alone, save for the company of his own picture. He was like a man who has been groping his way through difficult paths in the dark—uneasy, it may be, and nervous, but with no serious alarm. On a sudden, a storm-flash may reveal to him that he is on the very edge of a precipice or already ankle-deep in some bottomless morass. The sight of his own face, interpreted with all Morewood's penetrating insight and mastery of hand, had been a revelation to him. No more mercilessly candid messenger could have been found. Arguments he would have resisted or confuted; appeals to his own consciousness would have failed for want of experience; he could not affect to disbelieve the verdict of his own countenance. He had in all his life been a man who dealt plainly with himself; it was only in this last matter that the power, more than the will, to understand his own heart had failed him. His intellect now reasserted itself. He did not attempt to blink facts; he did not deny the truth of the revelation or seek to extenuate its force. He did not tell himself that the matter was a trifle, or that its effect would be transient. He recognized that he had fallen from the state of a priest vowed to Heaven, to that of a man whose whole heart and mind had gone out in love for a woman and were filled with her image. His judgment of himself was utterly reversed, his pre-suppositions confounded, his scheme of life wrecked; all this he knew for truth, unless indeed it might be that victory could still be his—victory after a struggle even to death; a struggle that had found no type or forecast in the mimic contests that had marked, almost without disturbing, his earlier progress on the road of his choice.

In the long hours that he sat gazing at the picture his mind was the scene of changing moods. At first the sense of horror and shame was paramount. He was aghast at himself and too full of self-abhorrence to do more than fight blindly away from what he could not but see. He would fain have lost his senses if only to buy the boon of ignorance. Then this mood passed. The long habit of his heart asserted itself, and he fell on his knees, no longer in horror, but in abasement and penitence. Now all his thought was for the sin he had done to Heaven and to his vow; but had he not learnt and taught, and re-learnt in teaching, that there was no sin without pardon, if pardon were sought? And for a moment, not peace, but the far-off possible hope and prospect of peace regained comforted his spirit. It might be yet that he would come through the dark valley, and gaze with his old eyes on the light of his life set in the sky.

But was his sin only against Heaven and his vow and himself? Is sin so confined? If Morewood had seen, had not others? Had not she seen? Would not the discovery he had made come to her also? Nay, had it not come? He had been blind; but had she? Was it not far more likely that she had not deceived herself as to the tendency of their friendship, nor dreamt that he meant anything except what his acts, words, and looks had so plainly—yes, to his own eyes now, so plainly declared? He looked back on her graciousness, her delight in his society, her unconcealed admiration for him. What meaning had these but one? What did she know of his vow? Why should she dream of anything save the happy ending of the story that flits before the half-averted eyes of a girl when she is with her lover? Even if she had heard of his vow, would they not all tell her it was a conceit of youth, a spiritual affectation, a thing that a wise counselor would tell him and her quietly to set aside? Did it not all point to this? He was not only a perjurer toward Heaven, but his sin had brought woe and pain to her he loved.

So he groaned in renewed self-condemnation. But what did that mean? And then an irresistible tide of triumph swept over him, obliterating shame and horror and remorse. She loved him. He had won. Be it good or evil, she was his! Who forbade his joy? Though all the world, aye, and all Heaven, were against him, nothing should stop him. Should he sin for naught? Should he not have the price of his soul? Should he not enjoy what he had bought so dearly? Enough of talking, and enough of reasoning! Passion filled him, and he knew no good nor evil save its satiety or hunger.

The mad mood passed, and there came a worthier mind. He sat and looked along the avenue of his life. He saw himself walking hand in hand with her. Now she was not the instrument of his pleasure, but the helper in his good deeds. By her sweet influence he was stronger to do well; his broader sympathies and fuller life made a servant more valuable to his Master; he would serve Heaven as well and man better, and, knowing the common joys of man, he would better minister to common pains. Who was he that he should claim to lead a life apart, or arrogate to himself an immunity and an independence other men had not? Man and woman created He them, and did it not make for good? And he sank back in his chair, with the picture of a life before him, blessed and giving blessings, and ending at last in an old age, when she would still be with him, when he should be the head and inspiration of a house wherein God's service was done, when he should see his son's sons following in his steps, and so, having borne his part, fall asleep, to wake again to an union wherein were no stain of earth and no shadow of parting.

From these musings he awoke with a shudder, as there came back to him many a memory of lofty pitying words, with which he had gently drawn aside the cloak of seemliness wherein some sinner had sought to wrap his sin. His dream of the perfect joint-life, what was it but a sham tribute to decency, a threadbare garment for the hideousness of naked passion? Had he taught himself to contemplate such a life, and shaped himself for it, it might be a worthy life—not the highest, but good for men who were not made for saints. But as it was, it seemed to him but a glazing over of his crime. Sternly there stood between him and it his profession and his pledge. If he would forsake the one and violate the other, by Heaven, he would do it boldly, and not seek to slink out by such self-cozening. At least he would not deceive himself again. If he sinned, he would sin openly to his own heart. There should be no compact: nothing but defeat or victory! And yet, was he right? It would be pitiful if for pride's sake, if for fear of the sneers of men, he were to kill her joy and defile his own soul with her heart's blood. People would laugh at the converted celibate—was it that he feared? Had he fallen so low as that? or was the shrinking he felt not rather the dread that his fall would be a stone of stumbling to others? for in his infatuation he had assumed to be an example. Was there no distinguishing good and evil? Could every motive and every act change form and color as you looked at it, and be now the counsel of Heaven, and now the prompting of Satan? How, then, could a man choose his path? In his bewilderment the darkness closed round him, and he groaned aloud.

It was late now, nearly midnight, and the house was quiet. Stafford walked to the open window and leant out, bending his tired head upon his hand. As he looked out he saw through the darkness Eugene and Ayre still sitting on the terrace. Ayre was talking.

"Yes," he was saying, "we are taught to think ourselves of a mighty deal of importance. How we fare and what we do is set before us as a thing about which angels rejoice or mourn. The state of our little minds, or souls, or whatever it is, is a matter of deep care to the Creator—the Life of the universe. How can it be? How are we more than minutest points in that picture in his mind, which is the world? I speak in human metaphor, as one must speak. In truth, we are at once a fraction, a tiny fraction—oh! what a tiny fraction—of the picture, and the like little jot of what it exists for. And does what comes to us matter very much—whether we walk a little more or a little less cleanly—aim a little higher or lower, if there is a higher and lower? What matter? Ah, Eugene, our parents and our pastors teach us vanity! To me it seems pitiful. Let us take our little sunshine, doing as little harm and giving as little pain as we may, living as long as we can, and doing our little bit of useful work for the ground when we are dead, if we did none for the world when we were living. If you cremate, you will deprive many people of their only utility."

Eugene gently laughed.

"Of course you put it as unattractively as you can."

"Yes; but I can't put it unattractively enough to be true. I used to fret and strive, and think archangels hung on my actions. There are none; and if there were, what would they care for me? I am a part of it, I suppose—a part of the Red King's dream, as Alice says. But what a little part! I do well if I suffer little and give little suffering, and so quietly go to help the cabbages."

"I don't think I believe it," said Eugene.

"I suppose not. It's hard to believe and impossible to disbelieve."

Stafford listened intently. Memories came back to him of books he had read and put behind him; books wherein Ayre had found his creed, if the thing could be called a creed. Was that true? Was he rending his soul for nothing? A day earlier such a thought would have been to him at once a torture and a sin. Now he found a strange comfort in it. Why strive and cry, when none watched the effort or heard the agony? Why torture himself? Why torture others? If the world were good, why was he not to have his part? If it were bad, might he not find a quiet nook under the wall, out of the storm? Why must he try to breast it? If Ayre was right, what a tragical farce his struggle was, what a perverse delusion, what an aimless flinging away of the little joy his little life could offer! If this were so, then was he indeed alone in the world—except for Claudia. Was his choice in truth between this world and the next? He might throw one away and never find the other.

Then he cursed the voice, and himself for listening to it, and fell again to vehement prayers and self-reproaches, trying to drown the clamor of his heart with his insistent petitions. If he could only pray as he had been wont to pray, he was saved. There lay a respite from thought and a refuge from passion. Why could he not abandon his whole soul to communion with God, as once he could, shutting out all save the sense of sin and the conviction of forgiveness? He prayed for power to pray. But, like the guilty king, he could not say Amen. He could not bind his wandering thoughts, nor dispel the forward imaginings of his distempered mind. He asked one thing, and in his heart desired another; he prayed, and did not desire an answer to his prayer; for when he tried to bow his heart in supplication, ever in the midst, between him and the throne before which he bent, came the form and the face and the voice he loved, and the temptation and the longing and the doubt. And he was tost and driven about through the livelong night till, in utter weariness, he fell on the floor and slept.

CHAPTER VII.

An Early Train and a Morning's Amusement.

It was still early when he awoke, weary, stiff, and unrefreshed, but with a conviction in his mind that had grown plain and strong in the mysterious way notions sometimes seem to gather force in hours of unconsciousness, and surprise us with their mature vigor when we awake. "I must go!" he kept muttering to himself; "I must go—go and think. I dare do nothing now." He hastily packed a hand bag, wrote a note for Eugene, asking that the rest of his luggage might be forwarded to an address he would send, went quietly downstairs, and, finding the door just opened, passed out unseen. He had three miles to walk to the station, but his restless feet brought him there quickly, and he had more than an hour to wait for the first train, at half-past eight. He sat down on the platform and waited. His capacity for thought and emotion seemed for the time exhausted. His thoughts wandered from one trivial matter to another, always eluding his effort to fix them. He found himself acutely studying the gang of laborers who were going by train to their day's work, and wondering how many pipes each of their carefully guarded matches would light, and what each carried in his battered tin drinking-bottle, remembering with a dreary sort of amusement that he had heard this same incurable littleness of thought settled on men condemned to death. Still, it passed the time, and he was surprised out of a sort of reverie by the clanging of the porter's inharmonious bell.

At the same moment a phaeton was rapidly driven up to the door of the station, and all the porters rushed to meet it.

"Label it all for London," he heard Eugene's voice say. "Four boxes, a portmanteau, and a hat-box. No, I'm not going—this lady and gentleman."

Kate, Haddington, and Eugene came through the ticket-office on to the platform. Stafford involuntarily shrank back.

"Just in time!" Eugene was saying; "though why the dickens you people will start at such an hour, I don't know. Haddington, I suppose, always must be in a hurry—never does for a rising man to admit he's got spare time. But you, Kate! Its positively uncomplimentary!"

He spoke lightly, but there was a troubled look on his face; and as Haddington went off to take the tickets he drew near to Kate, and said suddenly:

"You are determined on this, Kate?"

"On what?" she asked coldly.

"Why, to go like this—to bolt—it almost comes to that—leaving things as they are between us?"

"Why not?"

"And with Haddington?"

"Do you mean to insult me?"

"Of course not. But how do you think it must look to me? What do you imagine my course must be?"

"Really, Eugene, I see no need for this scene. I suppose your course will be to wait till I ask you to fulfill your promise, and then to fulfill it. You have no sort of cause for complaint."

Eugene could not resist a smile.

"You are sublime!" he said. Perhaps he would have said more, but at this moment, to his intense surprise, his eyes met Stafford's. The latter gave him a quick look, in obedience to which he checked his exclamation, and, making some excuse about a parcel due and not arrived, unceremoniously handed Kate to a carriage, bundled Haddington in after her, and walked rapidly to the front of the train, where he had just seen Stafford getting into a third-class compartment.

"What in the world's the meaning of this, my dear old boy?"

"I have left a note for you."

"That will explain?"

"No," said Stafford, with his unsparing truthfulness, "it will not explain."

"How fagged you look!"

"Yes, I am tired."

"You must go now, and like this?"

"I think that is less bad than anything else."

"You can't tell me?"

"Not now, old fellow. Perhaps I will some day."

"You'll let me know what you're doing? Hallo, she's off! And, Stafford, nothing ever between us?"

"Why should there be?" he answered, with some surprise. "But you know there couldn't be."

The train moved on as they shook hands, and Eugene retraced his steps to his phaeton.

"He's given her up," he said to himself, with an irrepressible feeling of relief. "Poor old fellow! Now —"

But Eugene's reflections were not of a character that need or would repay recording. He ought to have been ashamed of himself. I venture to think he was. Nevertheless, he arrived home in better spirits than a man has any right to enjoy when he has seen his mistress depart in a temper and his best friend in sorrow. Our spirits are not always obedient to the dictates of propriety. It is often equally in vain that we call them from the vasty deep, or try to dismiss them to it. They are rebellious creatures, whose only merit is their sincerity.

Sir Roderick Ayre allowed few things to surprise him, but the fact of any one deliberately starting by the early train was one of the few. In regard to such conduct, he retained all his youthful capacity for wonder. Surprise, however, gave way to unrestrained and indecent exultation when he learned that the early party had consisted of Kate and Haddington, and that Eugene himself had escorted them to the station. Eugene was in too good a temper to be seriously annoyed.

"I know it makes me look an ass," he said, as they smoked the after-breakfast pipe, "but I suppose that's all in the day's work."

"No doubt. It is the day's work," said Ayre; "but, oh, diplomatic young man, why didn't you tell us at breakfast that the pope had also gone?"

"Oh, you know that?"

"Of course. My man Timmins brings me what I may call a way-bill every morning, and against Stafford's name was placed '8.30 train.'"

"Useful man, Timmins," said Eugene. "Did he happen to add why he had gone?"

"There are limitations even to Timmins. He did not."

"You can guess?"

"Well, I suppose I can," answered Ayre, with some resentment.

"He's given it up, apparently."

"I don't know."

"He must have. Awfully cut up he looked, poor old chap! I was glad Kate and Haddington didn't see him."

"Poor chap! He takes it hard. Hallo! here's the *fons et origo mali*."

Morewood joined them.

"I have been," he said gravely, "rescuing my picture. That insipid lunatic had wrapped it up in brown paper, and put it among his socks in his portmanteau. I couldn't see it anywhere till I routed out the portmanteau. If it had come to grief I should have entered the Academy."

"Don't give way so," said Ayre; "it's unmanly. Control your emotions."

Eugene rose.

"Where are you going?"

Eugene smiled.

"This," said Ayre to Morewood, with a wave of his hand, "is an abandoned young man."

"It is," said Morewood. "Bob Territon is going rat-hunting, and proposes we shall also go. What say you?"

"I say yes," said Sir Roderick, with alacrity. "It's a beastly cruel sport."

"You have lost," said Morewood, as they walked away together.

"Wait a bit!" said his companion. "But, young Eugene! It's a pity that young man has no morals."

"Is that so?"

"Oh! not *simpliciter*, you know. *Secundum quid.*"

"*Secundum feminam*, in fact?"

"Yes; and I brought him up, too."

"'By their fruits ye shall know them.' But here's Bob and the terriers."

"Don't you fellows ever have a sister," said Bob, as he came up; "Claudia's just savage because the pope's gone. Can't get her morning absolution, you know."

"Are absolution and ablution the same word, Morewood?" asked Ayre.

"Don't know. Ask the Rector. He's sure to turn up when he hears of the rats."

"I think they must be—a sort of spiritual tub. But Morewood will never admit he's been educated. It detracts from his claim to genius."

Eugene, freed from this frivolous company, was not long in discovering Claudia's whereabouts. He felt like a boy released from school and, turning his eyes away from future difficulties, was determined to enjoy himself while he could. Claudia was seated on the lawn in complete idleness and, apparently, considerable discontent.

"Do your guests always scurry away without saying good-by to anybody, Mr. Lane?" she asked.

"I hope that you, at least, will not. But didn't Kate say good-by, or Haddington?"

"I meant Father Stafford, of course."

"Oh, he had to go. He sent an apology to you and all the party."

"Did he tell you why he had to go?"

"No," said Eugene, regarding her with covert attention.

"It's a pity if he's unaccountable. I like him so much otherwise."

"You don't like unaccountable people?"

Claudia seemed quite willing to let Stafford drop out of the conversation.

"No," she said; "I tolerate you, Mr. Lane, because I always know exactly what you'll do."

"Do you?" he asked, only moderately pleased. A man likes to be thought a little mysterious. No doubt Claudia knew that.

"I don't think you know what I am going to do now."

"What?"

"I'm going to ask you if you know why Father Stafford—"

"Oh, please excuse me, Mr. Lane. I can't speculate on your friend's motives. I don't profess to understand him."

This might be indifference; it sounded to Eugene very like pique.

"I thought you might know."

"Mr. Lane," said Claudia, "either you mean something or you don't. If the one, you're taking a liberty, and one entirely without excuse; if the other, you are simply tedious."

"I beg your pardon," said Eugene stiffly.

Claudia gave a little laugh.

"Why do you make me be so aggressive? I don't want to be. Was I awfully severe?"

"Yes, rather."

"I meant it, you know. But did you come quite resolved to quarrel? I want to be pleasant." And Claudia raised her eyes with a reproachful glance.

"In anger or otherwise, you are always delightful," said Eugene politely.

"I accept that as a diplomatic advance—not in its literal sense. After all, I must be nice to you. You're all alone this morning."

"Lady Claudia," said he gravely, "either you mean something or you do not. If the one—"

"Be quiet this moment!" she said, laughing.

He obeyed and lay back in his low chair with a sigh of content.

"Yes; never mind Stafford and never mind Kate. Why should we? They're not here."

"My silence is not to be taken for consent," said Claudia, "only it's too fine a day to spend in trying to improve you or, indeed, anybody else. But I shall not forget any of my friends."

Now up to this point Eugene had behaved tolerably well. It is, however, a dangerous thing to set yourself deliberately to study a lady's attractions. Like all other one-sided views of a subject, it is apt to carry you too far. The sun and the wind were playing about in Claudia's hair, her eyes were full of light, and her whole air, in spite of a genuine effort after demureness, conveyed to any self-respecting man an irresistible challenge to make himself agreeable if he could. Eugene's notions of making himself agreeable were, as may have been gathered, liberal; they certainly included more than can be considered strictly incumbent on young men in society. And, besides being polite, Eugene was also curious. It is one thing to silently suffer under a passion which a sense of duty forbids; such a position has its pleasures. The situation is altered when the idea dawns upon you that there is no reciprocity of graceful suffering; that, in fact, the lady may prefer somebody else. Eugene wanted to know where he stood.

"Shall you be sorry to leave here?" he asked.

"My feelings will be mixed. You see, Rickmansworth has actually consented to take me with him to his moor, and that will be great fun."

"Why, you don't go killing birds?"

"No, I don't kill birds."

"There'll be only a pack of men there."

"That's all. But I don't mind that—if the scenery is good."

"I believe you're trying to make me angry."

"Oh, no! I know Sir Roderick doesn't let you be angry. It's not good form."

"Have you no heart, Claudia?"

"I don't know. But I have a prefix."

"Have you, after ten years' friendship?"

Claudia laughed.

"You make me rather old. Were we friends when I was ten?"

"Oh, bother dates! I don't count by time?"

"Really, Mr. Lane, if you were anybody else I should call this absurd. It would be flattering you and myself to call it wrong."

"Why?"

"Because that would imply you were serious."

"Would it be wrong if I were?"

"Well, it would be generally considered so, under the circumstances."

"I don't care about that. I have endured it long enough. Oh, Claudia! don't you see?"

"I suppose so," thought Claudia, "I ought to crush him at this point. I think I'll wait a little bit, though."

"See what?" she said.

"Why, that—that—"

"Well?"

"Hang it! why is it always so abominably absurd? Why, that I love the ground you tread on, Claudia? Is this wretched thing to keep us apart!"

"Mr. Lane, you're magnificent; but isn't there a trifling assumption in your last remark?"

"How?"

"Well, you seemed—perhaps you didn't mean it—to imply that only that 'wretched thing' kept us apart. That's rather taking me for granted, isn't it?"

"Ah! you know I didn't mean it. But if things were different, could you—"

"A conditional proposal is a new fashion. Is that one of Sir Roderick's ideas?"

Eugene was at last angry. He was silent for a moment. Then he said:

"I see. I must congratulate you."

"On what?"

"On having bagged a brace—without accident to yourself. But I have had enough of it."

And without waiting for a reply to this very rude speech, he rose and flung himself across the lawn into the house.

Claudia seemed less angry than she ought to have been. She sat with a little smile for a moment, then she threw her hat in the air and caught it, then lay back, sighed gently, and murmured:

"Heigho! a brace means two, doesn't it? Who's the other? Oh! Mr. Haddington, I suppose. I didn't think he knew. Poor Eugene! He's very angry, or he'd never have been so rude. 'Bagged a brace!'"

And she actually laughed again, and then said "Heigho!" again.

Just at this moment Ayre came up the drive, looking very hot and very disgusted. Seeing Claudia, he came and sat down.

"Bob's rat-hunting's a mere fraud," he said. "I was there half an hour, and we only bagged a brace."

"What a curious coincidence!" exclaimed Claudia.

"How a coincidence!"

"Oh, nothing. Bagging a brace means killing two, doesn't it?"

"Yes. Why?"

"Oh, I wanted to know."

Ayre looked at her.

"Where's Eugene?"

"He was here just now, but he's gone into the house."

Ayre stroked his mustache meditatively.

"Did you want him?"

"No, not particularly. I thought I should find him here."

"You would if you'd come a little sooner."

"Ah! I'll go and find him."

"Yes, I should."

And off he went.

"It is really very pleasant," said Claudia, "to prevent Sir Roderick finding out things that he wants to find out. I think it does me credit—and it annoys him so very much. I will go and have a nice drive with Mrs. Lane, and see some old women. I feel as if I ought to do something proper."

And perhaps it was about time.

CHAPTER VIII

Stafford in Retreat, and Sir Roderick in Action.

When Stafford got into the train on his headlong flight from Millstead Manor, he had no settled idea of his destination, and he arrived in London without having made much progress toward a resolution. Not knowing what he wanted, he could not decide where he was most likely to find it. Did he want to forget or to think; to repent or to resolve? This is the alternative that presents itself to a mind puzzled to know whether its doubt is a concession to sin or a homage to reason. Stafford had been bred in a school widely different from that which treats all questions as open, and all to be referred to the verdict of the balance of expediency. Among other lessons, he had been taught a deep distrust of the instrument by which he was forced to guide his actions. But no training had succeeded in eradicating a strong mind's instinct of self-confidence, and if up till now he had committed no rebellion, it was because his reason had been rather a voluntary and eager helper than a captive or slave to the tribunal he distinguished from it by the name of conscience. With some surprise at himself—a surprise that now took the place of shame—he recognized that he was not ready to take everything for granted, that he must know that what he was flying from was in fact sin, not only that it might be. That it was sin he fully believed, but he would be sure. So much triumph his passion extorted from him as he paced irresolutely up and down the square in front of Euston, after seeing Kate and Haddington safely away, while the porter and cabman wondered why the traveler seemed not sure where he wanted to go. Of their wonder and their irreverent suggestions he was supremely careless.

No, he would not go back at once to his active work. Not only did his health still forbid that—and, indeed, last night's struggle seemed to him to have undone most of the good he had gained from the quiet of Millstead—but, what was more, he believed, above all, in the importance of the state of the pastor's own soul, and was convinced that his work would be weak and futile done under such conditions; that in theological language, there would be no blessing on it. When he had once reached that conclusion, his path was plain before him. He would go to the Retreat. This word Retreat has become familiar to those who study ecclesiastical items in the paper. But the Retreat Stafford had in his mind was not quite of the common kind. It had been founded by one of the leaders of his party, and was intended to serve the function of a spiritual casual ward, whither those who were for the moment at a loss might resort and find refuge until they had time to turn round. It was not a permanent home for any one. After his stay, the visitor returned to the world if he would; if he were finally disabled he was passed on to a permanent residence of another kind. The Retreat was a temporary refuge only. Sometimes it was full, sometimes it was empty; save for the Superintendent, as he was called; for religious terms were avoided, and a severe neutrality of description forbade the possibility of the Retreat itself seeming to take any side in the various mental battles for which it afforded a clear field, remote from interruption and from the bias alike of the world and of previous religious prepossessions. A man was entirely left to himself at the Retreat. Save at the dinner hour, no one spoke to him except the Superintendent. The rule of his office was that he should always be ready to listen on all subjects, and to talk on all indifferent subjects. Advice and exhortation were forbidden to him. If a man wanted the ordinary consolations of religion, his case was not the special case the Retreat was founded to meet. When nobody could help a man, and nothing was left for him but to go through with the struggle in his own soul, then he came to the Retreat. There he stayed till he reached some conclusion: that is, if he could reach one within a reasonable time; for the pretense of unconquerable hesitation was not received. When he arrived at his resolve, he went away: what the resolve was, and where he was going, whether to High or Low, to Rome or Islington, to Church or Dissent, or even to Mohammed or Theosophy, or what not, or nothing, nobody asked. Such a foundation had struck many devoted followers of the Founder as little better than a negation or an abdication. The Founder thought otherwise. "If forms and words are of any use to him, a man will never come," he said; "if he comes, let him alone." And it may be that this difference between the Founder and his disciples was due to the fact that the Founder believed that, given a fair field in any honest mind, his views must prevail, whereas the disciples were not so strong in faith.

It is very possible the disciples were right, in a way; but still the Founder's scheme now and then caught a great prize that the disciples would have lost through their overgreat meddling. The Founder would have repudiated the idea of differences in value between souls. But men sometimes act on ideas they repudiate, and with very good results.

Whatever the merits or demerits of the Retreat might be, it was just the place Stafford wanted. He shrank, almost with loathing, from the thought of exposing himself to well meant ministrations from men who were his inferiors: the theory of the equalizing effect of the sacred office, which appears to be held in great tranquillity by many who see the absurdity of parallel ideas applied in other spheres, was one of the fictions that proved entirely powerless over his mind at this juncture. He did not say to himself that fools were fools and blind men blind, whatever their office, degree, or profession, but he was driven to the Retreat by a thought that a brutal speaker might have rendered for him in those words without essential misrepresentation. Above all, he wanted quiet—time to understand the new forces and to estimate the good or evil of the new ideas.

Arriving there late in the evening of the same day on which he left Millstead, for the Retreat was situated on the borders of Exmoor and the journey from Paddington was long and slow, he was received by the Superintendent with the grave welcome and studious absence of questioning that was the rule of the house. The Superintendent was an elderly man, inclining to stoutness and of unyielding placidity. It was suspected that the Founder had taken pains to choose a man who would observe his injunction of not meddling with thorny questions the more strictly from his own inability to understand them.

"We are very empty just now," he said, with a sigh. Poor man! perhaps it was dull. "Only two, besides yourself."

"The fewer the better," said Stafford, with a smile, half in earnest, half humoring the genius of the place.

The Superintendent looked as if he might have said something on the other side but refrained, and, without more ado, made Stafford at home in the bare little room that was to serve him for sleeping and living. Stafford was full of weariness, and sank down on the bed with a sense of momentary respite. He would not begin to think till to-morrow.

Here we must leave him to wage his uncertain battle. When the visible and the invisible meet in the shock of strife about the soul of a man, who may describe the changes and chances of the fight? In the peace of his chosen solitude would he re-conquer the vision that the clouds had hidden from him? Or would the allurements of his earthly love be less strong because its dazzling incitements were no longer actually before his eyes? He had refused all aid and all alliance. He had chosen to try the issue alone and unbefriended. Was he strong enough?—strong enough to think on his love, and yet not to bow to it?—strong enough to picture to himself all its charms, only to refuse to gather them? Should he not have seized every aid that counsel and authority could offer him? Would he not find too late that his true strategy had been to fly, and not to challenge, the encounter? He had fancied he could be himself the impartial judge in his own cause, however vast the bribe that lay ready to his hand. The issue of his sojourn alone could tell whether he had misjudged his strength.

While Stafford mused and strove the world moved on, and with it that small fraction of it whose movements most nearly bore on the fortunes of the recluse.

The party at Millstead Manor was finally broken up by the departure of the Territons and of Morewood about a week after Stafford left. The cricket-match came off with great *éclat*; in spite of a steady thirteen from the Rector, who spent two hours in "compiling" it—to use the technical term—and of several catches missed by Sir Roderick, who was tried in vain in all positions in the field, the Manor team won by five wickets, and Bob Territon felt that his summer had been well spent. Ayre lingered on with Eugene, shooting the coverts till mid September, when the latter abruptly and perhaps rudely announced that he could not stand it any longer, and straightway took himself off to the Continent, sending a line to Stafford to apprise him of the fact, and another to Kate, to say he would have no address for the next month.

For a moment Sir Roderick was at a loss. He was tired of shooting; he hated yachting; the ordinary country-house visit was nothing but shooting in the daytime and unmitigated boredom in the evening. Really he didn't know what to do with himself. This alarming state of mind might have issued in some incongruous activity of a useful sort, had not he been rescued from it by the sudden discovery that he had a mission. This revelation dawned upon him in consequence of a note he received from Lord Rickmansworth. It appeared that that nobleman had very soon got tired of his moor, had resigned it into the eager hands of Bob Territon, and was now at Baden-Baden. This was certainly odd, and the writer evidently knew it would appear so; he therefore appended an explanation which was entirely satisfactory to Sir Roderick, but which is, happily, irrelevant to the purposes of this story. What is more to the purpose, it further appeared that Mrs. Welman, Kate Bernard's aunt, had discarded Buxton in favor of the same resort, and that Mr. Haddington, M. P., had also "proceeded" thither.

"They are at the Victoria," wrote Rickmansworth; "I am at the Badischerhof, and—[irrelevant matter]. I go about a good deal with them, but it's beastly slow. Haddington is all day in Kate's pocket, and Kate at best isn't amusing. But what's Lane up to? Do come out here, old fellow. I'll find you some amusement. Who do you think is here with—[more irrelevant matter]."

Sir Roderick was influenced in part, no doubt, by the irrelevant matter. But he also felt that what concerns us concerned him. He had come to a very definite conclusion that Kate Bernard ought not to marry Eugene Lane. He was also sure that unless something was done the marriage would take place. Kate did not care for Eugene, but the match was too good to be given up. Eugene would never face the turmoil necessary to break it off.

"I am the man," said Sir Roderick to himself. "I couldn't catch the parson, but if I can't catch Miss Kate, call me an ass!"

And he took train to Baden, sending off a wire to Morewood to join him if he could, for a considerable friendship existed between them. Morewood, however, wouldn't come, and Ayre was forced to make the journey in solitude.

"I thought I should bring him!" exclaimed Lord Rickmansworth triumphantly, as he received his friend on the platform, and conducted him to a very perfect drag which stood at the door. "Oh, you old thief!"

Rickmansworth was a tall, broad, reddish-faced young man, with a jovial laugh, infinite capacity for being amused at things not intrinsically humorous, and manners that he had tried, fortunately with imperfect success, to model on those of a prize-fighter. Ayre liked him for what he was, while shuddering at what he tried to be.

"I didn't come on that account at all," he said, "I came to look after some business."

"Get out!" said the Earl pleasantly; "do you think I don't know you?"

Ayre allowed himself to yield in silence. His motives were a little mixed; and, anyhow, it was not at the moment desirable to explain them. His vindication would wait.

In the afternoon he paid his call on Mrs. Welman. She was delighted to see him, not only as a man of social repute, but also because the good lady was in no little distress of mind. The arrangement between Kate and Eugene was, as a family arrangement, above perfection. Mrs. Welman was not rich, and like people who are not rich, she highly esteemed riches; like most women, she looked with favor on Eugene; the fact of Kate having some money seemed to her, as it does to most people, a reason for her marrying somebody who had more, instead of aiding in the beneficent work of a more equal distribution of wealth. But Kate was undeniably willful. She treated her engagement, indeed, as an absolutely binding and unbreakable tie—a fact so conclusively accomplished that it could almost be ignored. But she received any suggestion of a possible excess in her graciousness toward Haddington and her acceptance of his society, as at once a folly and an insult; and as she was of age and paid half the bills, all means of suasion were conspicuously lacking. Mrs. Welman was in a position exactly the reverse of the pleasant one; she had responsibility without power. It is true her responsibility was mainly a figment of her own brain, but its burden upon her was none the less heavy for that.

It must be admitted that Ayre's dealings with her were wanting in candor. Under the guise of family friendship, he led her on to open her mind to him. He extracted from her detailed accounts of long excursions into the outskirts of the forest, of numberless walks in the shady paths, of an expedition to the races (where perfect solitude can always be obtained), and of many other diversions which Kate and Haddington had enjoyed together, while she was left to knit "clouds" and chew reflections in the Kurhaus garden. All this, Ayre recognized, with lively but suppressed satisfaction, was not as it should be.

"I have spoken to Kate," she concluded, "but she takes no notice; will you do me a service?"

"Of course," said Ayre; "anything I can."

"Will you speak to Mr. Haddington?"

This by no means suited Ayre's book. Moreover, it would very likely expose him to a snub, and he had no fancy for being snubbed by a man like Haddington.

"I can hardly do that. I have no position. I'm not her father, or uncle, or anything of that sort."

"You might influence him."

"No, he'd tell me to mind my own business. To speak plainly, my dear lady, it isn't as if Kate couldn't take care of herself. She could stop his attentions to-morrow if she liked. Isn't it so?"

Mrs. Welman sadly admitted it was.

"The only thing I can do is to keep an eye on them, and act as I think best; that I will gladly do."

And with this very ambiguous promise poor Mrs. Welman was forced to be content. Whatever his inward view of his own meaning was, Ayre certainly fulfilled to the letter his promise of keeping an eye on them. Kate was at first much annoyed at his appearance; she thought she saw in him an emissary of Eugene. Sir Roderick tactfully disabused her mind of this notion, and, without intruding himself, he managed to be with them a good deal, and with Haddington alone a good deal more. Moreover, even when absent, he could generally have given a shrewd guess where they were and what they were doing. Without altogether neglecting the other claims at which Rickmansworth had hinted, and which resolved themselves into a long-standing and entirely platonic attachment, he yet devoted himself with zest and assiduity to his self-imposed task.

In its prosecution he contrived to make use of Rickmansworth to some extent. The young man was a hospitable soul, delighting in parties and picnics. Only consent to sit with him on his four-in-hand and let him drive you, and he cheerfully feasted you and all your friends. His acquaintance was large, and not, perhaps, very select. But Ayre insisted on the proper distinctions being observed, and was indebted to Rickmansworth's parties for many opportunities of observation. He was sure Haddington meant to marry Kate if he could; the scruples which had in some degree restrained his actions, though not his designs, at Millstead, had vanished, and he was pushing his suit, firmly and daringly ignoring the fact of the engagement. Kate did nothing to remind him of it that Ayre could see, but her behavior, on the other hand, convinced him that Haddington was to her only a second string, and that, unless compelled, she would not let Eugene go. She took occasion more than once to show him that she regarded her relation to Eugene as fully existent. No doubt she thought there was a chance that such words might find their way to Eugene's ears. It is hardly necessary to say they did not.

Watch as he might Ayre's chance was slow in coming. He knew very well that the fact of a young lady, deserted by him who ought to have been in attendance, consoling herself with a flirtation with somebody else, was not enough for him to go upon. He must have something more tangible than that. He did not, indeed, look for anything that would compel Eugene to act; he had no expectation and, to do him justice, no hope of that, for he knew Eugene would act on nothing but an extreme necessity. His hope lay in Kate herself. On her he was prepared to have small mercy; against her he felt justified in playing the very rigor of the game. But for a long while he had no opportunity of beginning the rubber. A fortnight wore away, and nothing was done. Ayre determined to wait on events no longer; he would try his hand at shaping them.

"I wonder if Rick is too great a fool?" he said to himself meditatively one morning, as he crossed one of the little bridges, and took his way to the Kurhaus in search of his friend. "I must try him."

He found Lord Rickmansworth alone, but quite content. It was one of his happy characteristics that he existed with delight under almost any circumstances. One of his team was lame, and a great friend of his was sulky and had sent him away, and yet he sat radiantly cheerful, with a large cigar in his mouth and a small terrier by his side, subjecting every lady who passed to a respectful and covert but none the less searching and severe examination.

"I say, Rick, have you seen Haddington lately?"

"Yes; he's gone down the road with Kate Bernard to play tennis, or some such foolery."

"With Kate?"

"Rather! Didn't expect anything else, did you?"

"Does he mean to marry that girl?" asked Ayre, with a face of great innocence, much as if it had just occurred to him.

"Well, he can't, unless she chucks old Eugene over."

"Will she, do you think?"

"Well, I'm afraid not. I've got some money on that they're never married, but I don't see my way to handling it."

"Much?"

"Well, no; about twopence-halfpenny—a fancy bet."

"I'm glad it's nothing, because I want you to help me, and you couldn't have if you had anything on; besides, you shouldn't bet on such things."

"Oh, I'm not going to meddle with the thing. It's enough work to prevent one's self getting married, without troubling about other people. But I rather like you telling me not to bet on it!"

"She wouldn't suit Eugene."

"No; lead him the devil of a life."

"She don't care for him."

"Not a straw."

"Then, why don't she break it off?"

"Ah, you innocent?" said Rickmansworth, with a broad grin. "Never heard of such a thing as money in the case, did you? Where have you been these last five-and-forty years?"

"Your raillery's a little fatiguing, Rick, if you don't mind my saying so."

"Say anything you like, old chap, as long as it isn't swearing. That's *verbot* here—penalty one mark—see regulations. You must go outside, if you want to curse, barring of course you're a millionaire and like to make a splash."

"Rick, Rick, you do not amuse me. I do not belong to the Albatross Club."

"No; over age," replied his companion blandly, and chuckled violently.

"I like to score off old Ayre, you know," he said, in reporting the episode afterward. "He thinks himself smart."

"But look here. I want you to do this: you go to Haddington and stir him up; tell him to bustle along; tell him Kate is fooling him, and make him put it to her—yes or no."

"Why? it's not my funeral!"

"Is that your latest American? I wish you'd find native slang; we used in my day; but I'll tell you why. It's because she's keeping him on till she sees what Eugene'll do. She's treating Eugene shamefully."

"Oh, stow all that! Eugene is not so remarkably strict, you know." And Lord Rickmansworth winked.

"Well, we'll leave that out," said Ayre smiling. "Tell him it's treating *him* shamefully."

"That's more the ticket. But what if she says 'No'?"

"If she says 'No' right out, I'm done," said Ayre. "But will she?"

"The devil only knows!" said Lord Rickmansworth.

"Do you think you won't bungle it?"

"Do you take me for an ass? I'll make him move, Ayre; he shall give her a chaste salute before the day's out. Old Eugene's no better than he should be, but I'll see him through."

Ayre thought privately that his companion had perhaps other motives than love for Eugene: perhaps family feelings, generally dormant, had asserted themselves; but he had the wisdom not to hint at this.

"If you can frighten him, he'll press it on."

"Do you think I might lie a bit?"

"No, I shouldn't lie. It's awkward. Besides, you know you wouldn't do it, and you couldn't if you tried."

"I'll stir him up," reiterated Rickmansworth. "Give me my prayer-book and parasol, and I'll go and find him."

Ayre ignored what he supposed to be the joke buried in this saying, and saw his friend off on his errand, repeating his instructions as he went.

What Lord Rickmansworth said to Mr. Haddington has never, as the newspapers put it, transpired. But ever since that date Sir Roderick has always declared that Rick is not such a fool as he looks. Certainly the envoy was well pleased with himself when he rejoined his companion at dinner, and after imbibing a full glass of champagne, said:

"To-night, my worthy old friend, you will see."

"Did he bite?"

"He bit. That fellow's no fool. He saw Kate's game when I pointed it out."

"Will he stand up to her?"

"Rather! going to hold a pistol to her head."

"I wonder what she'll say?"

"That's your lookout. I've done my stage."

Ayre was nearer excitement than he had been for a long while. After dinner he could not rest. Refusing to accompany Rickmansworth to the entertainment the latter was bound for, he strolled out into the quiet walks outside the Kurhaus, which were deserted by visitors and peopled only by a few frugal natives, who saved their money and took the music of the band from a cheap distance. But surely some power was fighting for him, for before he had gone a hundred yards he saw on one of the seats in front of him two persons whom the light of the moon clearly displayed as Kate and Haddington. At Baden there is a little hillside—one path runs at the bottom, another runs along the side of the hill, halfway up. Ayre hastily diverted his steps into the upper path. A minute's walk brought him directly behind the pair. Trees hid him from them; a seat invited him. For a moment he struggled. Then, *rubesco referens*, he sat down and deliberately listened. With the sophisms by which he sought to

87

justify this action, we have no concern; perhaps he was not in reality much concerned about them. But what he heard had its importance.

"I have been more patient than most men," Haddington was saying.

"You have no right to speak in that way," Kate protested; "it's—it's not respectful."

"Kate, have we not got beyond respect?"

"I hope not," said Sir Roderick to himself.

"I mean," Haddington went on, "there is a point at which you must face realities. Kate, do you love me?"

Ayre leant forward and peered through the bushes.

"I will not break my engagement."

"That is no answer."

"I can't help it. I have been taught—"

"Oh, taught! Kate, you know Lane; you know what he is. You saw him with Lady—"

"You're very unkind."

"And for his sake you throw away what I offer?"

"Won't you be patient?"

"Ah, you admit—"

"No, I don't!"

"But you can't deny it. Now you make me happy."

The conversation here became so low in tone that Ayre, to his vast disgust, was unable to overhear it. The next words that reached his ear came again from Haddington.

"Well, I will wait—I will wait three months. If nothing happens then, you will break it off?"

A gentle "Yes" floated up to the eavesdropper.

"Though why you want him to break it off rather than yourself, I don't know."

"He doesn't appreciate her morality," reflected Ayre, with a chuckle.

"Kate, we are promised to one another? secretly, if you like, but promised?"

"I'm afraid it's very wrong."

"Why, he deliberately insulted you!"

The tones again became inaudible; but after a pause there came a sound that made Ayre almost jump.

"By Jove!" he whispered in his excitement. "Confound these trees! Was it only her hand, or—"

"Then I have your promise, dear?"

"Yes; in three months. But I must go in. Aunt will be angry."

"You won't let him win you over?"

"He has treated me badly; but I don't want it said I jilted him."

They had risen by now.

"You ask such a lot of me," said Haddington.

"Ah! I thought you said you loved me. Can't you wait three months?"

"I suppose I must. But, Kate, you are sincere with me? Tell me you love me."

Again Ayre leant forward. They had began to walk away, but now Haddington stopped, and laying his hand on Kate's arm, detained her. "Say you love me," he said again.

"Yes, I love you!" said Kate, with commendable confusion, and they resumed their walk.

"What is her game?" Ayre asked himself. "If she means to throw Eugene over, why doesn't she do it right out? I don't believe she does. She's afraid he'll throw her over. And, by Jove! she fobbed that fool off again! We're no further forward than we were. If he makes trouble about this she'll deny the whole thing. Miss Bernard is a lady of talent. But—no, can I? Yes, I will. Rather than let her win, I'll step in. I'll go and see her to-morrow. We shall neither of us be in a position to reproach the other. But I'll see what I can do. But Haddington! To think she should get round him again!"

CHAPTER IX.

The Battle of Baden.

Lord Rickmansworth was enjoying himself. Over and above the particular pleasures for whose sake he had come to Baden, he relished intensely the new attitude in which he found himself standing toward Ayre. Throughout their previous acquaintance it had been Rickmansworth who was eager and excited, Ayre who applied the cold water. Now the parts were reversed, and the younger man found great solace in jocosely rallying his senior on his unwonted zeal and activity. Ayre accepted his friend's jocosity and his own excitement with equal placidity. Reproaches had never stirred him to exertion; ridicule would not stop him now. He took leave to add himself to the materials for slightly contemptuous amusement that the world had hitherto afforded him, and he found his own absurd actions a very sensible addition to his resources. He realized why people who never act on impulse and never do uncalled-for things are not only dull to others, but suffer boredom themselves. However the Millstead love-affairs affected the principal actors, there can be no question that they relieved Sir Roderick Ayre from *ennui* for a considerable number of months and exercised a very wholesome effect on a man who had come to take pride in his own miserable incapacity for honest emotion.

He rose the next morning as nearly with the lark as could reasonably be expected; more nearly with the lark than the domestic staff of the Badischerhof at all approved of. Was not Kate Bernard in the habit of taking the waters at half-past seven? And in solitude? For Haddington's devotion was not allowed by him to interfere with that early ride which is so often a mark of legislators, and an assertion, I suppose, of the strain on their minds that might be ignored or doubted if not backed up by some such evidence. The strain, of course, followed Haddington to Baden; it was among his most precious appurtenances; and Ayre, relying upon it, had little doubt that he could succeed in finding Kate alone and unprotected.

He was not deceived. He found Kate just disposing of her draught, and an offer of his company for a stroll was accepted with tolerable graciousness. Kate distrusted him, but she thought there was use in keeping on outwardly good terms; and she had no suspicion of his shameless conduct the night before. Ayre directed their walk to the very same seat on which she and Haddington had sat. As they passed, either romance or laziness suggested to Kate that they should sit down. Ayre accepted her proposal without demur, asked and obtained leave for a cigarette, and sat for a few moments in apparent ease and vacancy of mind. He was thinking how to begin.

"Ought one ever to do evil that good may come?" he did begin, a long way off.

"Dear me, Sir Roderick, what a curious question! I suppose not."

"I'm sorry; because I did evil last night, and I want to confess."

"I really don't want to hear," said Kate, in some alarm. There's no telling what men will say when they become confidential, and Kate's propriety was a tender plant.

"It concerns you."

"Me? Nonsense! How can it?"

"In order to serve a friend, I did a—well—a doubtful thing."

Kate was puzzled.

"You are in a curious mood, Sir Roderick. Do you often ask moral counsel?"

"I am not going to ask it. I am, with your kind permission, going to offer it."

"You are going to offer me moral counsel?"

"I thought of taking that liberty. You see, we are old friends."

"We have known one another some time."

Ayre smiled at the implied correction.

"Do you object to plain speaking?"

"That depends on the speaker. If he has a right, no; if not, yes."

"You mean I should have no right?"

"I certainly don't see on what ground."

"If not an old friend of yours, as I had hoped to be allowed to rank myself, I am, anyhow, a very old friend of Eugene's."

"What has Mr. Lane to do with it?"

"As an old friend of his—"

"Excuse me, Sir Roderick; you seem to forget that Mr. Lane is even more than an old friend to me."

"He should be, no doubt," said Ayre blandly.

"I shall not listen to this. No old friendship excuses impertinence, Sir Roderick."

"Pray don't be angry. I have really something to say, and—pardon me—you must hear it."

"And what if I refuse?"

"True; I did wrong to say 'must.' You are at perfect liberty. Only, if you refuse, Eugene must hear it."

Kate paused. Then, with a laugh, she said:

"Perhaps I am taking it too gravely. What is this great thing I must hear?"

"Ah! I hoped we could settle it amicably. It's merely this: you must release Eugene from his engagement."

Kate did not trouble to affect surprise. She knew it would be useless.

"Did he send you to tell me this?"

"You know he didn't."

"Then whose envoy are you? Ah! perhaps you are Claudia Territon's chosen knight?"

"Not at all," said Ayre, still unruffled. "I have had no communication with Lady Claudia—a fact of which you have no right to affect doubt."

"Then what do you mean?"

"I mean you must release Eugene."

"Pray tell me why," asked she calmly, but with a calm only obtained after effort.

"Because it is not usual—and in this matter it seems to me usage is right—it is not usual for a young lady to be engaged to two men at once."

"You are merely insolent. I will wish you good-morning."

"I am glad you understand my insinuation. Explanations are so tedious. Where are you going, Miss Bernard?"

"Home."

"Then I must tell Eugene?"

"Tell him what you like." But she sat down again.

"You are engaged to Eugene?"

"Of course."

"You are also engaged to Spencer Haddington."

"It's untrue; you know it's untrue. Are you an old woman, to think a girl can't speak to a man without being engaged to him?"

"I must congratulate you on your liberality of view, Miss Bernard. I had hardly given you credit for it. But you know it isn't untrue. You are under a promise to give Haddington your hand in three months: not, mark you, a conditional promise—an absolute promise."

"That is not a happy guess."

"It's not a guess at all. No doubt you mean it to be conditional. He understood, and you meant him to understand, it as an absolute promise."

"How dare you accuse me of such things?"

"Nothing short of absolute knowledge would so far embolden me."

"Absolute knowledge?"

"Yes, last night."

Kate's rage carried her away. She turned on him in fury.

"You listened!"

"Yes, I listened."

"Is that what a gentleman does?"

"As a rule, it is not."

"I despise you for a mean dastard! I have no more to say to you."

"Come, Miss Bernard, let us be reasonable. We are neither of us blameless."

"Do you think Eugene would listen to such a tale? And such a person?"

"He might and he might not. But Haddington would."

"What could you tell him?"

"I could tell him that you're making a fool of him—keeping him dangling on till you have arranged the other affair one way or the other. What would he say then?"

Kate knew that Haddington was already tried to the uttermost. She knew what he would say.

"You see I could—if you'll allow me the metaphor—blow you out of the water."

"You daren't confess how you got the knowledge."

"Oh, dear me, yes," said Ayre, smiling. "When you're opening a blind man's eyes he doesn't ask after your moral character. You must consider the situation on the hypothesis that I am shameless."

Kate was not strong enough to carry on the battle. She had fury, but not doggedness. She burst into tears.

"If I were doing all you say, whose fault was it?" she sobbed. "Didn't Eugene treat me shamefully?"

"If he flirted a little, it was in part your fault. If you had flirted a little with Haddington, I should have said nothing. But this—well, this is a little strong."

"I am a very unhappy girl," said Kate.

"It isn't as if you cared twopence for Eugene, you know."

"No, I hate him!" said Kate, unwisely yielding to anger again.

"I thought so. And you will do what I ask?"

"If I don't, what will you do?"

"I shall write to Eugene. I shall see Haddington; and I shall see your aunt. I shall tell them all that I know, and how I know it. Come, Miss Bernard, don't be foolish. You had better take Haddington."

"I know it's all a plot. You're all fighting in that little creature's interest."

"Meaning—?"

"Claudia Territon. But if I can help it, Eugene shall never marry her."

"That's another point."

"His friend Father Stafford will have to be considered there."

"Do not let us drift into that. Will you write?"

"To whom?"

"To Eugene."

Kate looked at him with a healthy hatred.

"And you will tell Haddington he needn't wait those three months?"

"I suppose you're proud of yourself now!" she broke out. "First eavesdropping, and then bullying a girl!"

"I'm not at all proud of myself, and I am, if you'd believe it, rather sorry for you."

"I shall take care to let your friends know my opinion of you."

"Certainly—with any details you think advisable. Have I your promise? Is it any use struggling any longer? This scene is so very unpleasant."

"Won't you give me a week?"

"Not a day!"

Kate drew herself up with a sort of dignity.

"I despise you and your schemes, and Eugene Lane, and Claudia Territon, and all your crew!" she allowed herself to say.

"But you promise?"

"Yes, I promise. There! Now, may I go?"

Ayre courteously took off his hat, and stood on one side, holding it in his hand and bowing slightly as she swept indignantly by him.

"I'll give her a day to tell Haddington, and three days to tell Eugene. Unless she does, I must go through it all again, and it's damnably fatiguing. She's not a bad sort—fought well when she was cornered. But I couldn't let Eugene do it—I really couldn't. Ugh! I'll go back to breakfast."

Kate was cowed. She told Haddington. Let us pass over that scene. She also wrote to Eugene, addressing the letter to Millstead Manor. Eugene was not at Millstead Manor; and if Ayre had hastily assumed

Father Stafford

that his *fiancée* would be in possession of his address, was it her business to undeceive him? She was by no means inclined to do one jot more than fulfill the letter of her bond—whereby it came to pass that Eugene did not receive the letter for nearly two months and did not know of his recovered liberty all that time. For Haddington, in his joy, easily promised silence for a little while; it seemed only decent; and even Ayre could not refuse to agree with him that, though Eugene must be told, nobody else ought to be until Eugene had formally signified his assent to the lady's transfer. Ayre could not take upon himself, on his friend's behalf, the responsibility of dispensing with this ceremony, though he was sure it would be a mere ceremony.

As for Ayre himself, when his task was done he straightway fled from Baden. He was a hardened sinner, but he could not face Mrs. Welman.

It was, however, plainly impossible to confine the secret so strictly as to prevent it coming to the knowledge of Lord Rickmansworth. Indeed he had a right to know the issue, for he had been a sharer in the design; and accordingly, when he also left Baden and betook himself to his own house to spend what was left of the autumn, he carried locked in his heart the news of the fresh development. On the whole he observed the injunction of silence urgently laid upon him by Ayre with tolerable faithfulness. But there are limits to these things, and it never entered Rickmansworth's head that his sister was included among the persons who were to remain in ignorance till the matter was finally settled. He met Claudia at the family reunion at Territon Park in the beginning of October, and when she and he and Bob were comfortably seated at dinner together, among the first remarks he made—indeed, he was brimming over with it— was:

"I suppose you've heard the news, Clau?"

What with one thing—packing and unpacking, traveling, perhaps less obvious troubles—Lady Claudia was in a state which, if it manifested itself in a less attractive person, might be called snappish.

"I never hear any news," she answered shortly.

98

"Well, here's some for you," replied the Earl, grinning. "Kate has chucked Eugene over."

"Nonsense!" But she started and colored, all the same.

"I suppose you were at Baden and saw it all, and I wasn't!" said Rickmansworth, with ponderous satire. "So we won't say any more about it."

"Well, what do you mean?"

"No; never mind! It doesn't matter—all a mistake. I'm always making some beastly blunder—eh, Bob?" and he winked gently at his appreciative brother.

"Yes, you're an ass, of course!" said Bob, entering into the family humor.

"Good thing I've got a sister to keep me straight!" pursued the Earl, who was greatly amused with himself. "Might have gone about believing it, you know."

Claudia was annoyed. Brothers are annoying at times.

"I don't see any fun in that," she said.

Lord Rickmansworth drank some beer (beer was the Territon drink), and maintained silence.

The butler came in with his satellite, swept away the beer and the other *impedimenta*, and put on dessert. The servants disappeared, but silence still reigned unbroken.

Claudia arose, and went round to her brother's chair. He was ostentatiously busy with a large plum.

"Rick, dear, won't you tell me?"

"Tell you! Why, it's all nonsense, you know."

"Rick, dear!" said Claudia again, with her arm around his neck.

He was going to carry on his jest a little further, when he happened to look at her.

"Why, Clau, you look as if you were almost—"

"Never mind that," she said quickly. "Oh! do tell me."

"It is quite true. She's written breaking it off, and has accepted Haddington. But it's a secret, you know, till they've heard from Eugene, at all events. Must hear in a day or two."

"Is it really true?

"Of course it is."

Claudia kissed him, and suddenly ran out of the room.

The brothers looked at one another.

"I hope that's all right?" said the elder questioningly.

"I expect so," answered the younger. "But, you see, you don't quite know where to have Eugene."

"I shall know where to have him, if necessary."

"You'd better keep your hoof out of it, old man," said Bob candidly.

Pursuing his train of thought, Rickmansworth went on:

"Must have been rather a queer game at Millstead?"

"Yes. There was Eugene and Kate, and Claudia and the parson, and old Ayre sticking his long nose into it."

"Trust old Ayre for that; and is it a case?"

"Well, now Kate's out of it, I expect it is, only you don't know where to have Eugene. And there's the parson."

"Yes; Ayre told us a bit about him. But she doesn't care for him?"

"She didn't tell him so—not by any means," said Bob; "and I bet he's far gone on her."

"She can't take him."

"Good Lord! no."

Though how they proposed to prevent it did not appear.

"Think Lane'll write to her?"

"He ought to, right off."

"Queer girl, ain't she?"

"Deuced!"

"Old Ayre! I say, Bob, you should have seen the old sinner at Baden."

"What? with Kate?"

"No; the other business."

And they plunged into matters with which we need not concern ourselves, and proceeded to rend and destroy the character of that most respectable, middle-aged gentleman, Sir Roderick Ayre. The historian hastens to add that their remarks were, as a rule, entirely devoid of truth, with which general comment we may leave them.

CHAPTER X.

Mr. Morewood is Moved to Indignation.

When Morewood was at work he painted portraits, and painted them uncommonly well. Of course he made his moan at being compelled to spend all his time on this work. He was not, equally of course, in any way compelled, except in the sense that if you want to make a large income you must earn it. This is the sense in which many people are compelled to do work, which they give you to understand is not the most suited to their genius, and it must be admitted that, although their words are foolish, not to say insincere, yet their deeds are sensible. There can be no mistake about the income, and there often is about the genius. Morewood, whose eccentricity stopped short of his banking account, painted his portraits like other people, and only deviated into landscape for a month in the summer, with the unfailing result of furnishing a crop of Morewoodesque parodies on Mother Nature that conclusively proved the fates were wiser than the painter.

This year it so chanced that he chose the wilds of Exmoor for the scene of his outrages. He settled down in a small inn and plied his brush busily. Of course he did not paint anything that the ordinary person cared to see, or in the way in which it would appear to such person. But he was greatly pleased with his work; and one day, as he threw himself down on a bank at noon and got out his bread and cheese, he was so carried away, being by nature a conceited man, as to exclaim:

"My head of Stafford was the best head done these hundred years; and that's the best bit of background done these hundred and fifty!"

The frame of the phrase seemed familiar to him as he uttered it, and he had just succeeded in tracing it back to the putative parentage of Lord Verulam, when, to his great astonishment, he heard Stafford's voice from the top of the bank, saying:

"As I am in your mind already, Mr. Morewood, I feel my bodily appearance less of an intrusion on your solitude."

"Why, how in the world did you come here?"

The spot was within ten miles of the Retreat, and part of Stafford's treatment for himself consisted of long walks; but he only replied:

"I am staying near here."

"For health, eh?"

"Yes—for health."

"Well, I'm glad to see you. How are you? You don't look very first-class."

Stafford came down the bank without replying, and sat down. He was, in spite of it being the country and very hot, dressed in his usual black, and looked paler and thinner than ever.

"Have some lunch?"

Stafford smiled.

"There's only enough for one," he said.

"Nonsense, man!"

"No, really; I never take it."

A pause ensued. Stafford seemed to be thinking, while Morewood was undoubtedly eating. Presently, however, the latter said:

"You left us rather suddenly at Millstead."

"Yes."

"Sent for?"

"You of all men know why I went, Mr. Morewood."

"If you don't mind my admitting it, I do. But most people are so thin-skinned."

"I am not thin-skinned—not in that way. Of course you know. You told me."

"That head?"

"Yes; you did me a service."

"Well, I think I did, and I'm glad to hear you say so."

"Why?"

"Shows you've come to your senses," said Morewood, rapidly recovering from his lapse into civility.

Stafford seemed willing, even anxious, to pursue the subject. The *regimen* at the Retreat was no doubt severe.

"What do you mean by coming to my senses?"

"Why, doing what any man does when he finds he's in love— barring a sound reason against it."

"And that is?"

"Try his luck. You needn't look at me. I've tried my luck before now, and it was damned bad luck. So here I am, a musty old curmudgeon; and there's Ayre, a snarling old cur!"

"I don't bore you about it?"

"No, I like jawing."

"Well then, I was going to say, of course you don't know how it struck me."

"Yes, I do, but I don't think any the better of it for that."

"You knew about my vow? I suppose you think that—"

"Bosh? Yes, I do. I think all vows bosh; but without asking you to agree to that, though I think I did ask the Bishop of Bellminster to, I do say this one is utter bosh. Why, your own people say so, don't they?"

"My own people? The people I suppose you mean don't say so. I took a vow never to marry—there were even more stringent terms— but that's enough."

"Well?"

"A vow," continued Stafford, "that you won't marry till you want to is not the same as a vow never to marry."

"No. I think I could manage the first sort."

"The first sort," said Stafford, with a smile, "is nowadays a popular compromise."

"I detest compromises. That's why I liked you."

"You're advising me to make one now."

"No, I advise you to throw up the whole thing."

"That's because you don't believe in anything?"

"Yes, probably."

"Suppose you believed all I believe and had done all I had?"

"How do you mean?"

"You believed what a priest believes—in heaven and hell—the gaining God and the losing him—in good and evil. Supposing you, believing this, had given your life to God, and made your vow to him—had so proclaimed before men, had so lived and worked and striven! Supposing you thought a broken vow was death to your own soul and a trap to the souls of others—a baseness, a treason, a desertion—more cowardly than a soldier's flight—as base as a thief's purloining—meaning to you and those who had trusted you the death of good and the triumph of evil?"

He sat still, but his voice was raised in rapid and intense utterance; he gazed before him with starting eyes.

"All that," he went on, "it meant to me—all that and more—the triumph of the beast in me—passion and desire rampant—man forsaken and God betrayed—my peace forever gone, my honor forever stained. Can't you see? Can't you see?"

Morewood rose and paced up and down.

"Now—now can you judge? You say you knew—did you know that?"

"Do you still believe all that?"

"Yes, all, and more than all. For a moment—a day—perhaps a week, I drove myself to doubt. I tried to doubt—I rejoiced in it. But I cannot. As God is above us, I believe all that."

"If you break this vow you think you will be—?"

"The creature I have said? Yes—and worse."

"I think the vow utter nonsense," said Morewood again.

"But if you thought as I think, then would your love—yes, and would a girl's heart, weigh with you?"

Morewood stood still.

"I can hardly realize it," he said, "in a man of your brain. But—"

"Yes?" said Stafford, looking at him almost as if he were amused, for his sudden outburst had left him quite calm.

"If I believed that, I'd cut off my hand rather than break the vow."

"I knew it!" cried Stafford, "I knew it!"

Morewood was touched with pity.

"If you're right," he said, "it won't be so hard to you. You'll get over it."

"Get over it?"

"Yes; what you believe will help you. You've no choice, you know."

Stafford still wore a look of half-amusement.

"You have never felt belief?" he asked.

"Not for many years. That's all gone."

"You think you have been in love?"

106

"Of course I have—half a dozen times."

"No more than the other," said Stafford decisively.

Morewood was about to speak, but Stafford went on quickly:

"I have told you what belief is—I could tell you what love is; you know no more the one than the other. But why should I? I doubt if you would understand. You think you couldn't be shocked. I should shock you. Let it be. I think I could charm you, too. Let that be."

A pause followed. Stafford still sat motionless, but his face gradually changed from its stern aspect to the look that Morewood had once caught on his canvas.

"You're in love with her still?" he exclaimed.

"Still?"

"Yes. Haven't you conquered it? I'm a poor hand at preaching, but, by Jove! If I thought like you, I'd never think of the girl again."

"I mean to marry her," said Stafford quietly. "I have chosen."

Morewood was in very truth shocked. But Stafford's morals, after all, were not his care.

"Perhaps she won't have you," he suggested at last, as though it were a happy solution.

Stafford laughed outright.

"Then I could go back to my priesthood, I suppose?"

"Well—after a time."

"As a burglar who is caught before his robbery goes back to his trade. As if it made the smallest difference—as if the result mattered!"

"I suppose you are right there."

"Of course. But she will have me."

"Do you think so?"

"I don't doubt it. If I doubted it, I should die."

"I doubt it."

"Pardon me; I dare say you do."

"You don't want to talk about that?"

"It isn't worth while. I no more doubt it than that the sun shines. Well, Mr. Morewood, I am obliged to you for hearing me out. I had a curiosity to see how my resolution struck you."

"If you have told me the truth, it strikes me as devilish. I'm no saint; but if a man believes in good, as you do, by God, he oughtn't to trample it under foot!"

Stafford took no notice of him, He rose and held out his hand. "I'm going back to London to-morrow," he said, "to wait till she comes."

"God help you!" said Morewood, with a sudden impulse.

"I have no more to do with God," said Stafford.

"Then the devil help you, if you rely on him!"

"Don't be angry," he said, with a swift return of his old sweet smile. "In old days I should have liked your indignation. I still like you for it. But I have made my choice."

"'Evil, be thou my good.' Is that it?"

"Yes, if you like. Why talk about it any more? It is done."

He turned and walked away, leaving Morewood alone to finish his forgotten lunch.

He could not get the thought of the man out of his mind all day. It was with him as he worked, and with him when he sat after dinner in the parlor of his little inn, with his pipe and whisky and water. He was so full of Stafford that he could not resist the impulse to tell somebody else, and at last he took a sheet of paper.

"I don't know if he's in town," he said, "but I'll chance it;" and he began:

"DEAR AYRE:

"By chance down here I met the parson. He is mad. He painted for me the passion of belief—which he said I hadn't and implied I couldn't feel. He threatened to paint the passion of love, with the same assertion and the same implication. He is convinced that if he breaks his vow (you remember it, of course) he'll be worse than Satan. Yet his face is set to break it. You probably can't help it, and wouldn't if you could, for you haven't heard him. He's going to London. Stop him if you can before he gets to Claudia Territon. I tell you his state of mind is hideous.

"Yours,

"A. MOREWOOD."

This somewhat incoherent letter reached Sir Roderick Ayre as he passed through London, and tarried a day or two in early October. He opened it, read it, and put it down on the breakfast-table. Then he read it again, and ejaculated.

"Talk about madness! Why, because Stafford's mad—if he is mad—must our friend the painter go mad too? Not that I see he is mad. He's only been stirring up old Morewood's dormant piety."

He lit his cigar, and sat pondering the letter.

"Shall I try to stop him? If Claudia and Eugene have fixed up things it would be charitable to prevent him making a fool of himself. Why the deuce haven't I heard anything from that young rascal? Hullo! who's that?"

He heard a voice outside, and the next moment Eugene himself rushed in.

"Here you are!" he said. "Thought I should find you. You can't keep away from this dirty old town."

"Where do you spring from?" asked Ayre.

"Liverpool. I found the Continent slow, so I went to America. Nothing moving there, so I came back here. Can you give me breakfast?"

Ayre rang the bell, and ordered a new breakfast; as he did so he took up Morewood's letter and put it in his pocket.

Eugene went on talking with gay affectation about his American experiences. Only when he was through his breakfast did he approach home topics.

"Well, how's everybody?"

Ayre waited for a more definite question.

"Seen the Territons lately?"

"Not very. Haven't you?"

"No. They weren't over there, you know. Are they alive?"

"My young friend, are you trying to deceive me? You have heard from at least one of them, if you haven't seen them?"

"I haven't—not a line. We don't correspond: not *comme il faut*."

"Oh, you haven't written to Claudia?"

"Of course not."

"Why not?"

"Why should I?"

"Let us go back to the previous question. Have you heard from Miss Bernard?"

"Why probe my wounds? Not a single line."

"Confound her impudence! she never wrote?"

"I don't know why she should. But in case she ought, I'm bound to say she couldn't."

"Why not? She said she would; she said so to me."

"She couldn't have said so. You must have misunderstood her. I left no address, you know; and I had no difficulty in eluding interviewers—not being a prize-fighter or a minor poet."

Sir Roderick smiled.

"Gad! I never thought of that. She held me, after all."

"What on earth are you driving at?"

"If there's one thing I hate more than another, it's a narrative; but I see I'm in for it. Sit still and hold your tongue till I'm through with it."

Eugene obeyed implicitly; and Ayre, not without honest pride, recounted his Baden triumph.

"And unless she's bolder than I think, you'll find a letter to that effect."

Eugene sat very quiet.

"Well, you don't seem overpleased, after all. Wasn't I right?"

"Quite right, old fellow. But, I say, is she in love with Haddington?"

"Ah, there's your beastly vanity? I think she is rather, you know, or she'd never have given herself away so."

"Rum taste!" said Eugene, whose relief at his freedom was tempered by annoyance at Kate's insensibility. "But I'm awfully obliged. And, by Jove, Ayre, it's new life to me!"

"I thought so."

Eugene had got over his annoyance. A sudden thought seemed to strike him.

"I say, does Claudia know?"

"Rickmansworth's sure to have told her on the spot. She must have known it a month; and what's more, she must think you've known it a month."

"Inference that the sooner I show up the better."

"Exactly. What, are you off now? Do you know where she is?"

"I shall send a wire to Territon Park. Rick's sure to be there if she isn't, and I'll go down and find out about it."

"Wait a minute, will you? Have you heard from your friend Stafford lately?"

A shadow fell on Eugene's face.

"No. But that's over. Must be, or he'd never have bolted from Millstead."

Ayre was silent a moment. Morewood's letter told him that Stafford had set out to go to Claudia. What if he and Eugene met? Ayre had not much faith in the power of friendship under such circumstances.

"I think, on the whole, that I'd better show you a letter I've had," he said. "Mind you, I take no responsibility for what you do."

"Nobody wants you to," said Eugene, with a smile. "We all understand that's your position."

Ayre flung the letter over to him and he read it.

"Oh, by Jove, this is the devil!" he exclaimed, jumping off the writing-table, where he had seated himself.

"So Morewood seems to think."

"Poor old fellow! I say, what shall I do? Poor old Stafford! Fancy his cutting up like this."

"It's kind of you to pity him."

"What do you mean? I say, Ayre, you don't think there is anything in it?"

"Anything in it?"

"You don't think there's any chance that Claudia likes him?"

"Haven't an idea one way or the other," said Ayre rather disingenuously.

Eugene looked very perturbed.

"You see," continued Ayre, "it's pretty cool of you to assume the girl is in love with you when she knew you were engaged to somebody else up to a month ago."

"Oh, damn it, yes!" groaned Eugene; "but she knew old Stafford had sworn not to marry anybody."

"And she knew—of course she knew—you both wanted to marry her. I wonder what she thought of both of you!"

"She never had any idea of the sort about him. About me she may have had an inkling."

"Just an inkling, perhaps," assented Sir Roderick.

"The worst of it is, you know, if she does like me I shall feel a brute, cutting in now. Old Stafford knew I was engaged too, you know."

"It all serves you right," observed Ayre comfortingly. "If you must get engaged at all, why the deuce couldn't you pick the right girl?"

"Fact is, I don't show up over well."

"You don't; that is a fact."

"Ayre, I think I ought to let him have his shot first."

"Bosh! why, as like as not she'd take him! If it struck her that he was chucking away his immortal soul and all that for her sake, as like as not she'd take him. Depend upon it, Eugene, once she caught the idea of romantic sin, she'd be gone—no girl could stand up against it."

"It is rather the sort of thing to catch Claudia's fancy."

"You cut in, my boy," continued Ayre, "Frendship's all very well—"

"Yes, 'save in the office and affairs of love!'" quoted Eugene, with a smile of scorn at himself.

"Well, you'd better make up your mind, and don't mount stilts."

"I'll go down and look round. But I can't ask her without telling her or letting him tell her."

"Pooh! she knows."

"She doesn't, I tell you."

"Then she ought to. You're a nice fellow! I slave and eavesdrop for you, and now you won't do the rest yourself. What the deuce do you all see in that parson? If I were your age, and thought Claudia Territon would have me, it would take a lot of parsons to put me on one side."

"Poor old Charley!" said Eugene again. "Ayre, he shall have his shot."

"Meanwhile, the girl's wondering if you mean to throw her over. She's expected to hear from you this last month. I tell you what: I expect Rick'll kick you when you do turn up."

"Well, I shall go down and try to see her: when I get there I must be guided by circumstances."

"Very good. I expect the circumstances will turn out to be such that you'll make love to Claudia and forget all about Stafford. If you don't——"

"What?"

"You're an infernally cold-blooded conscientious young ruffian, and I never took you for that before!"

And Ayre, more perturbed about other people's affairs than a man of his creed had any business to be, returned to the *Times* as Eugene went to pursue his errand.

CHAPTER XI.

Waiting Lady Claudia's Pleasure

Stafford had probably painted his state of mind in colors somewhat more startling than the reality warranted. When a man is going to act against his conscience, there is a sort of comfort in making out that the crime has features of more striking depravity than an unbiased observer would detect; the inclination in this direction is increased when it is a question of impressing others. Sin seems commonplace if we give it no pomp and circumstance. No man was more free than Stafford from any conscious hypocrisy or posing, or from the inverted pride in immorality that is often an affectation, but also, more often than we are willing to allow, a real disease of the mind. But in his interview with Morewood he had yielded to the temptation of giving a more dramatic setting and stronger contrasts to his conviction and his action than the actual inmost movement of his mind justified. It was true that he was determined to set action and conviction in sharp antagonism, and to follow an overpowering passion rather than a belief that he depicted as no less dominant. Had his fierce words to Morewood reproduced exactly what he felt, it may be doubted whether the resultant of two forces so opposite and so equal could have been the ultimately unwavering intention that now possessed him. In truth, the aggressive strength of his belief had been sapped from within. His efforts after doubt, described by himself as entirely unsuccessful, had not in reality been without result. They had not issued in any radical or wholesale alteration of his views. He was right in supposing that he would still have given as full intellectual assent to all the dogmas of his creed as formerly; the balance of probability was still in his view overwhelmingly in their favor. But it had come to be a balance of probability—not, of course, in the way in which a man balances one account of an ordinary transaction against another, and decides out of his own experience of how things happen—Stafford had not lost his mental discrimination so completely—but in the sense that he had appealed to reason, and thus admitted the jurisdiction of reason in matters which he had formerly proclaimed as outside the province of that sort of reasoning that governs other intellectual questions. In the result, he was left under the influence of a persuasion, not under the dominion of a command; and the former failed to withstand an assault that the latter might well have enabled him to repulse. He found himself able to forget what he believed, though not to disbelieve it; his convictions could be postponed, though not expelled; and in representing his mind as the present battle-ground of equal and opposite forces, he had rather expressed what a preacher would reveal as the inner truth of his struggle than what he was himself conscious of as going on within him. It is likely enough that his previous experience had made him describe his own condition rather in the rhetoric of the pulpit than in the duller language of a psychological narrative. He had certainly given Morewood one false impression, or rather, perhaps Morewood had drawn one false though natural inference for himself. He thought of Stafford, and his letter passed on the same view to Eugene, as of a man suffering tortures that passed enduring. Perhaps at the moment of their interview such was the case: the dramatic picture Stafford had drawn had for the moment terrified afresh the man who drew it. His normal state of mind, however, at this time was not unhappy. He was wretched now and then by effort; he was tortured by the sense of sin when he remembered to be. But for the most part he was too completely conquered by his passion to do other than rejoice in it. Possessed wholly by it, and full of an undoubting confidence that Claudia returned his love, or needed only to realize it fully to return it fully, he had silenced all opposition, and went forth to his wooing with an exultation and a triumph that no transitory self-judgments could greatly diminish. Life lay before him, long and full and rich and sweet. Let trouble be what it would, and right be what it might, life and love were in his own hands. The picture of a man giving up all he thought worth having, driven in misery by a force he could not resist to seek a remedy that he despaired of gaining—a remedy which, even if gained, would bring him nothing but fresh pain—this picture, over which Eugene was mourning in honest and perplexed friendship, never took form as a true presentment of himself to the man it was supposed to embody. If Eugene had known this, he would probably have felt less sympathy and more rivalry, and would have assented to Ayre's view of the situation rather than doubtingly maintained his own. A man may sometimes change himself more easily than he can persuade his friends to recognize the change.

Stafford left the Retreat the morning after his meeting with Morewood, feeling, he confessed to himself, as if he had taken a somewhat unfair advantage of its hospitality. The result of his sojourn there, if known to the Founder, might have been a trial of that enthusiast's consistency to his principles, and Stafford was glad to be allowed to depart, as he had come, unquestioned. He came straight to London, and turned at once to the task of finding Claudia as soon as he could. The most likely quarter for information was, he thought, Eugene Lane or his mother; and on the afternoon of his arrival in town—on the same day, that is, as Eugene had surprised Sir Roderick at breakfast—he knocked at the door of Eugene's house in Upper Berkeley Street, and inquired if Eugene were at home. The man told him that Mr. Lane had returned only that morning, from America, he believed, and had left the house an hour ago, on his way to Territon Park; he added that he believed Mr. Lane had received a telegram from Lord Rickmansworth inviting him to go down. Mrs. Lane was at Millstead Manor.

Stafford was annoyed at missing Eugene, but not surprised or disturbed to hear of his visit to Territon Park. Eugene did not strike him as a possible rival. It may be doubted whether in his present frame of mind he would have looked on any man's rivalry as dangerous, but of course he was entirely ignorant of the new development of affairs, and supposed Eugene to be still the affianced husband of Miss Bernard. The only way the news affected him was by dispelling the slight hope he had entertained of finding that Claudia had already returned to London.

He went back to his hotel, wrote a single line to Eugene, asking him to tell him Claudia's address, if he knew it, and then went for a walk in the Park to pass the restless hours away. It was a dull evening, and the earliest of the fogs had settled on the devoted city. A small drizzle of rain and the thickening blackness had cleared the place of saunterers, and Stafford, who prolonged his walk, apparently unconscious of his surroundings, had the dreary path by the

Serpentine nearly to himself. As the fog grew denser and night fell, the spot became a desert, and its chill gloom began to be burdensome even to his prepossessed mind. He stopped and gazed as far as the mist let him over the water, which lay smooth and motionless, like a sheet of opaque glass; the opposite bank was shrouded from his view, and imagination allowed him to think himself standing on the shore of some almost boundless lake. Seen under such conditions, the Serpentine put off the cheerful vulgarity of its everyday aspect, and exercised over the spirit of the watcher the same fascination as a mountain tarn or some deep, quick-flowing stream. "Come hither and be at rest," it seemed to whisper, and Stafford, responsive to the subtle invitation, for a moment felt as if to die in the thought of his mistress would be as sweet as to live in her presence, and, it might be, less perilous. At least he could be quiet there. His mind traveled back to a by-gone incident of his parochial life, when he had found a wretched shop-boy crouching by the water's edge, and trying to screw his courage up for the final plunge. It was a sordid little tragedy—an honest lad was caught in the toils of some slatternly Jezebel; she had made him steal for her, had spent his spoil, and then deserted him for his "pal"—his own familiar friend. Adrift on the world, beggared in character and fortune, and sore to the heart, he had wandered to the edge of the water, and listened to its low-voiced promises of peace. Stafford had stretched forth his hand to pluck him from his doom and set him on his feet; he prevailed on the lad to go home in his company, and the course of a few days proved once again that despair may be no more enduring than delight. The incident had almost faded from his memory, but it revived now as he stood and looked on the water, and he recognized with a start the depths to which he was in danger of falling. The invitation of the water could not draw him to it till he knew Claudia's will. But if she failed him, was not that the only thing left? His desire had swallowed up his life, and seemed to point to death as the only alternative to its own satisfaction. He contemplated this conclusion, not with the personal interest of a man who thought he might be called to act upon it,—Claudia would rescue him from that,—but with a theoretical certainty that if by any chance the staff on which he leant should break, he would be in no other mind than that from which he had rescued his miserable shop-boy. Death for love's sake was held up in poetry and romance as a thing in some sort noble and honorable; as a man might die because he could not save his country, so might he because he could not please his lady-love. In old days, Stafford, rigidly repressing his aesthetic delight in such literature, had condemned its teaching with half-angry contempt, and enough of his former estimate of things remained to him to prevent him regarding such a state of mind as it pictured as a romantic elevation rather than a hopeless degradation of a man's being. But although he still condemned, now he understood, if not the defense of such an attitude, at least the existence of it. He might still think it a folly; it no longer appeared a figment. A sin it was, no doubt, and a degradation, but not an enormity or an absurdity; and when he tried again to fancy his life without Claudia, he struggled in vain against the growing conviction that the pictures he had condemned as caricatures of humanity had truth in them, and that it might be his part to prove it.

With a shiver he turned away. Such imaginings were not good for a man, nor the place that bred them. He took the shortest cut that led out of the Park and back to the streets, where he found lights and people, and his thoughts, sensitive to the atmosphere round him, took a brighter hue. Why should he trouble himself with what he would do if he were deceived in Claudia? He knew her too well to doubt her. He had pushed aside all obstacles to seek her, and she would fly to meet him; and he smiled at himself for conjuring up fantasies of impossible misfortune, only to enjoy the solace of laying them again with the sweet confidence of love. He passed the evening in the contemplation of his happiness, awaiting Eugene's reply to his note with impatience, but without disquiet.

This same letter was, however, the cause of very serious disquiet to the recipient, more especially as it came upon the top of another troublesome occurrence. Rickmansworth had welcomed Eugene to Territon Park with his usual good nature and his usual absence of effusion. In fact, he telegraphed that Eugene could come if he liked, but he, Rickmansworth, thought he'd find it beastly slow. Eugene went, but found, to his dismay, that Claudia was not there. Some mystery hung over her non-appearance; but he learned from Bob that her departure had been quite impromptu, —decided upon, in fact, after his telegram was received,—and that she was staying some five miles off, at the Dower House, with her aunt, Lady Julia, who occupied that residence.

Eugene was much annoyed and rather uneasy.

"It looks as if she didn't want to see me," he said to Bob.

"It does, almost," replied Bob cheerfully. "Perhaps she don't."

"Well, I'll go over and call to-morrow."

"You can if you like. *I* should let her alone."

Very likely Bob's words were the words of wisdom, but when did a lover—even a tolerably cool-headed lover like Eugene—ever listen to the words of wisdom? He went to bed in a bad temper. Then in the morning came Stafford's letter, and of course Eugene had no kind of doubt as to the meaning of it. Now, it had been all very well to be magnanimous and propose to give his friend a chance when he thought the pear was only waiting to drop into his hand; magnanimity appeared at once safe and desirable, and there was no strong motive to counteract Eugene's love for Stafford. Matters were rather different when it appeared that the pear was not waiting to drop—when, on the contrary, the pear had pointedly removed itself from the hand of the plucker, and seemed, if one may vary the metaphor, to have turned into a prickly pear. Eugene still believed that Claudia loved him; but he saw that she was stung by his apparent neglect, and perhaps still more by the idea that in his view he had only to ask at any time in order to have. When ladies gather that impression, they think it due to their self-respect to make themselves very unpleasant, and Eugene did not feel sure how far this feeling might not carry Claudia's quick, fiery nature, more especially if she were offered a chance of punishing Eugene by accepting a suitor who was in many ways an object of her admiration and regard, and came to her with an indubitable halo of romance about him. Eugene felt that his consideration for Stafford might, perhaps, turn out to be more than a graceful tribute to friendship; it might mean a real sacrifice, a sacrifice of immense gravity; and he did what most people would do—he reconsidered the situation.

The matter was not, to his thinking, complicated by anything approaching to an implied pledge on his part. Of course Stafford had not looked upon him as a possible rival; his engagement to Kate Bernard had seemed to put him *hors de combat*. But he had been equally entitled to regard Stafford as out of the running; for surely Stafford's vow was as binding as his promise. They stood on an equality: neither could reproach the other—that is to say, each had matter of reproach against the other, but his mouth was closed. There was then only friendship—only the old bond that nothing was to come between them. Did this bond carry with it the obligation of standing on one side in such a case as this? Moreover, time was precious. If he failed to seek out Claudia that very day, she, knowing he was at Territon Park, would be justly aggrieved by a new proof of indifference or disrespect. And yet, if he were to wait for Stafford, that day must go by without his visit. Eugene had hitherto lived pleasantly by means of never asking too much of himself, and in consequence being always tolerably equal to his own demands upon himself. Quixotism was not to be expected of him. A nice observance of honor was as much as he would be likely to attain to; and friendship would be satisfied if he gave the doubtful points against himself.

He sat down after breakfast, and wrote a long letter to Stafford.

After touching very lightly on Stafford's position, and disclaiming not only any right to judge, but also any inclination to blame, he went on to tell in some detail the change that had occurred in his own situation, avowed his intention of gaining Claudia's hand if he could, clearly implied his knowledge that Stafford's heart was set on the same object, and ended with a warm declaration that the rivalry between them did not and should not alter his love, and that, if unsuccessful, he could desire to be beaten by no other man than Stafford. He added more words of friendship, told Stafford that he should try his luck as soon as might be, and that he had Rickmansworth's authority to tell him that, if he saw proper to come down for the same purpose, his coming would not be regarded as an intrusion by the master of the house.

Then he went and obtained the authority he had pledged, and sent his servant up to London with the letter, with instructions to deliver it instantly into Stafford's own hand. His distrust in the integrity of the postmaster's daughter in such a matter prevented his sending any further message by the wires than one requesting Stafford to be at home to receive his letter between twelve and one, when his messenger might be expected to arrive.

With a conscience clear enough for all practical purposes, he then mounted his horse, rode over to the Dower House, and sent in his card to Lady Julia Territon. Lady Julia was probably well posted up; at any rate, she received him with kindness and without surprise, and, after the proper amount of conversation, told him she believed he would find Claudia in the morning-room. Would he stay to lunch? and would he excuse her if she returned to her occupations? Eugene prevaricated about the lunch, for the invitation was obviously, though tacitly, a contingent one, and conceded the lady's excuses with as respectable a show of sincerity as was to be expected. Then he turned his steps to the morning-room, declining announcement, and knocked at the door.

"Oh, come in," said Claudia, in a tone that clearly implied, "if you won't let me alone and stay outside."

"Perhaps she doesn't know who it is," thought Eugene, trying to comfort himself as he opened the door.

CHAPTER XII.

Lady Claudia is Vexed with Mankind.

Of course she knew who it was, and her uninviting tone was a result of her knowledge. We are yet awaiting a systematic treatise on the psychology of women; perhaps they will some day be trained highly enough to analyze themselves. Until this happens, we must wait; for no man unites the experience and the temperament necessary. This could be proved, if proof were required; but, happily, proof of assertions is not always required, and proof of this one would lead us into a long digression, bristling with disputable matter, and requiring perhaps hardly less rare qualities than the task of writing the treatise itself. The modest scribe is reduced to telling how Claudia behaved, without pretending to tell why she behaved so, far less attempting to group her under a general law. He is comforted in thus taking a lower place by the thought that after all nobody likes being grouped under general laws—it is more interesting to be peculiar—and that Claudia would have regarded such an attempt with keen indignation; and by the further thought that if you once start on general laws, there's no telling where you will stop. The moment you get yours nicely formulated, your neighbor comes along with a wider one, and reduces it to a subordinate proposition, or even to the humiliating status of a mere example. Now even philosophers lose their temper when this occurs, while ordinary mortals resort to abuse. These dangers and temptations may be conscientiously, and shall be scrupulously, avoided.

Eugene advanced into the room with all the assurance he could muster; he could muster a good deal, but he felt he needed it every bit, for Claudia's aspect was not conciliatory. She greeted him with civility, and in reply to his remark that being in the neighborhood he thought he might as well call, expressed her gratification and hinted her surprise at his remembering to do so. She then sat down, and for ten minutes by the clock talked fluently and resolutely about an extraordinary variety of totally uninteresting things. Eugene used this breathing-space to recover himself. He said nothing, or next to nothing, but waited patiently for Claudia to run down. She struggled desperately against exhaustion; but at last she could not avoid a pause. Eugene's generalship had foreseen that this opening was inevitable. Like Fabius he waited, and like Fabius he struck.

"I have been so completely out of the world—out of my own world—for the last month that I know nothing. Didn't even have my letters sent on."

"Fancy!" said Lady Claudia.

"I wish I had now."

Claudia was meant to say "Why?" She didn't, so he had to make the connection for himself.

"I found one letter waiting for me that was most important."

"Yes?" said Claudia, with polite but obviously fatigued interest.

"It was from Miss Bernard."

"Fancy not having her letters sent on!"

"You know what was in that letter, Lady Claudia?"

"Oh, yes; Rickmansworth told me. I don't know if he ought to have. I am so very sorry, Mr. Lane."

"From not getting the letter, I didn't know for a month that I was free. I needn't shrink from calling it freedom."

"As you were in America, it couldn't make much difference whether you knew or not."

"I want you to know that I didn't know."

"Really you are very kind."

"I was afraid you would think—"

"Pray, what?" asked Claudia, in suspiciously calm tones.

Eugene was conscious he was not putting it in the happiest possible way; however, there was nothing for it but to go on now.

"Why, that—why, Claudia, that I shouldn't rush to you the moment I was free."

Claudia was sitting on a sofa, and as he said this Eugene came up and leant his hands on the back of it. He thought he had done it rather well at last. To his astonishment, she leapt up.

"This is too much!" she cried.

"Why, what?" exclaimed poor Eugene.

"To come and tell me to my face that you're afraid I've been crying for you for a month past!"

"Of course I don't mean—"

"Do I look very ill and worn?" demanded Claudia, with elaborate sarcasm. "Have I faded away? Make your mind easy, Mr. Lane. You will not have another girl's death at your door."

Eugene so far forgot himself as to stare at the ceiling and exclaim, "Good God!"

This appeared to add new fuel to the flame.

"You come and tell a girl—all but in words tell her—she was dying for love of you when you were engaged to another girl; dying to hear from you; dying to have you propose to her! And when she's mildly indignant you use some profane expression, just as if you had stated the most ordinary facts in the world! I am infinitely obliged for your compassion, Mr. Lane."

"I meant nothing of the sort. I only meant that considering what had passed between us—"

"Passed between us?"

"Well, yes at Millstead, you know."

"Are you going to tell me I said anything then, when I knew you were engaged to Kate? I suppose you will stop short of that?"

Eugene wisely abandoned this line of argument. After all, most of the talking had been on his side.

"Why will you quarrel, Claudia? I came here in as humble a frame of mind as ever man came in."

"Your humility, Mr. Lane, is a peculiar quality."

"Won't you listen to me?"

"Have I refused to listen? But no, I don't want to listen now. You have made me too angry."

"Oh, but do listen just a little—"

Claudia suddenly changed her tone—indeed, her whole demeanor.

"Not to-day," she said beseechingly; "really, not to-day. I won't tell you why; but not to-day."

"No time like the present," suggested Eugene.

"Do you know there is something you don't allow for in women?"

"So it seems. What is that?"

"Just a little pride. No, I will not listen to you!" she added with an imperious little stamp of her foot, and a relapse into hostility.

"May I come again?"

"I don't know."

Eugene was not a patient man. He allowed himself a shrug of the shoulders.

"Are you about to congratulate me on having 'bagged' another?"

"You're entirely hopeless to-day, and entirely charming!" he said. "If any girl but you had treated me like this, I'd never come near her again."

Claudia looked daggers.

"Pray don't make me an exception to your usual rule."

"As it is, I shall go away now and come back presently. You may then at least listen to me. That's all I've asked you to do so far."

"I am bound to do that. I will some day. But do go now."

"I will directly; but I want to speak to you about something else."

"Anything else in the world! And on any other subject I will be—charming—to you. Sit down. What is it?"

"It's about Stafford."

"Your friend Father Stafford? What about him?"

"He's coming down here."

"Oh, how nice! It will be a pleasant ref—resource."

Eugene smiled.

"Don't mind saying what you mean—or even what you don't mean; that generally gives people greater pleasure."

"You're making me angry again."

"But what do you think he's coming for?"

"To see you, I suppose."

"On the contrary. To see you."

"Pray don't be absurd."

"It's gospel truth, and very serious. He is in love with you. No—wait, please. You must forgive my speaking of it. But you ought to know."

"Father Stafford?"

"No other."

"But he—he's not going to marry anybody. He's taken a vow."

"Yes. He's going to break it—if you'll help him."

"You wouldn't make fun of this. Is it true?"

"Yes, it's desperately true. Now, I'm not going to tell you any more, or say anything more about it. He'll come and plead his own cause. If you'd treated me differently, I might have stopped him. As it is, he must come now."

"Why do you assume I don't want him to come?"

"I assume nothing. I don't know whether you'll make him happy or treat him as you've treated me."

"I shan't treat him as I've treated you, Eugene; is he—is he very unhappy about it?"

"Yes, poor devil!" said Eugene bitterly. "He's ready to give up this world and the next for you."

"You think that strange?"

Eugene shook his head with a smile.

> "'A man had given all other bliss
> And all his worldly worth,'"

he quoted. "Stafford would give more than that. Good-morning, Lady Claudia."

"Good-by," she said. "When is he coming?"

"To-day, I expect."

"Thank you."

"Claudia, if you take him, you'll let me know?"

"Yes, yes."

She seemed so absent and troubled that he left her without more, and made his way to his horse and down the drive, without giving a thought to the contingent lunch.

"She'll marry me if she doesn't marry him," he thought. "But, I say, I did make rather an ass of myself!" And he laughed gently and ruefully over Claudia's wrath and his own method of wooing. He would have laughed much the same gentle and rueful laugh over his own hanging, had such an unreasonable accident befallen him.

So far as the main subject of the interview was concerned, Claudia was well pleased with herself. Her indignation had responded very satisfactorily to her call upon it and had enabled her to work off on Eugene her resentment, not only for his own sins, but also for annoyances for which he could not fairly be held responsible. A patient lover must be a most valuable safety-valve. And although Eugene was not the most patient of his kind, Claudia did not think that she had put more upon him than he was able to bear—certainly not more than he deserved to bear. She would have dearly loved the luxury of refusing him, and although she had not been able to make up her mind to this extreme measure, she had, at least, succeeded in infusing a spice of difficulty into his wooing. She was so content with the aspect of affairs in this direction that it did not long detain her thoughts, and she found herself pondering more on the disclosure Eugene had made of Stafford's feelings than on his revelation of his own. It is difficult, without the aid of subtle distinctions, to say exactly what degree of surprise she felt at the news. She must, no doubt, have seen that Stafford was greatly attracted to her, and probably she would have felt that the description of his state of mind as that of a man in love only erred to the extent that a general description must err when applied to a particular case. But she was both surprised and disturbed at hearing that Stafford intended to act upon his feelings, and the very fact of her power having overcome him did him evil service in her thoughts. The secret of his charm for her lay exactly in the attitude of renunciation that he was now abandoning. She had been half inclined to fall in love with him just because there was no question of his falling in love with her. Her feelings toward Eugene, which lay deeper than she confessed, had prevented her actually losing her heart, or doing more than contemplate the picture of her romantic passion, banned by all manner of awful sanctions, as a not uninteresting possibility. By abandoning his position Stafford abandoned one great source of strength. On the other hand, he no doubt gained something. Claudia was not insensible to that aspect of the case which Ayre had apprehended would influence her so powerfully. She did perceive the halo of romance; and the idea of an Ajax defying heavenly lightning for her sake had its attractiveness. But Ayre reasoning, as a man is prone and perhaps obliged to do, from himself to another, had omitted to take account of a factor in Claudia's mind about the existence of which, even if it had been suggested to him, he would have been profoundly skeptical. Ayre had never been able, or at least never given himself the trouble, to understand how real a thing Stafford's vow had been to him, and what a struggle was necessary before he could disregard it. He would have been still more at a loss to appreciate the force which the same vow exercised over Claudia. Stafford himself had strengthened this feeling in her. Although the subject of celibacy, and celibacy by oath, had not been discussed openly between them, yet in their numerous conversations Stafford had not failed to respond to her sympathetic invitations so far as to give himself full liberty in descanting on the excellences of the life he had chosen for himself. Every word he had spoken in its praise now rose to condemn its betrayal. And Claudia, who had been brought up in entire removal from the spirit which made Ayre and Eugene treat Stafford's vow as one of the picturesque indiscretions of devotion, was unable to look upon the breaking of it in any other light than that of a falsehood and an act of treachery. Religion was to her a series of definite commands, and although her temperament was not such as enabled or led her to penetrate beneath the commands to the reason of them, or emboldened her to rely on the latter rather than the former, she had never wavered in the view that at least these commands may and should be observed, and that, above all, by a man whose profession it was to inculcate them. This much of genuine disapproval of Stafford's conduct she undoubtedly felt; and there it would be pleasant to leave the matter. But in the commanding interest of truth it must be added that this genuine disapproval was, unconsciously perhaps to herself, strengthened by more mundane feelings, which would, if analyzed, have been resolved into a sense of resentment against Stafford. He had come to her, as it were, under false pretenses. Relying on his peculiar position, she had allowed herself, without scruple, a freedom and expansion in her relations toward him that she would have condemned, though perhaps not abstained from, had he stood exactly where other men stood; and she felt that, if charged with encouraging him and fostering a delusion in his mind, her defense, though in reality a good one, was not one which the world would accept as justifying her. She could not openly plead that she had flirted with him, because she had never thought he would flirt with her; or allowed him to believe she entertained a deeper regard for him than she did because he could be supposed to feel none for her. Yet that was the truth; and perhaps it was a good defense. And Claudia was resentful because she could not defend herself by using it, and her resentment settled upon the ultimate cause of her perplexities.

When Eugene got back to Territon Park he was received by the brothers with unaffected interest. They were passing the morning in an exhaustive medical inspection of the dogs, but they left even this engrossing occupation, and sauntered out to meet him.

"Well, what luck?" asked Rickmansworth.

"The debate is adjourned," answered Eugene.

"Did Clau make herself agreeable?"

"Well, no; in fact she made herself as disagreeable as she knew how."

"Raised Cain, did she?" inquired Bob sympathetically.

"Something of the sort; but I think it's all right."

"You play up, old man," said Bob.

"Well, but what the devil are we to do with this parson?" Lord Rickmansworth demanded. "He'll be here after lunch, you know. You are an ass, Eugene, to bring him down!"

"I'm not quite sure, you know, that he won't persuade her."

"Why didn't you settle it this morning?"

"My dear fellow, she was impossible this morning."

"Oh, bosh!" said his lordship. "Now I'll tell you what you ought to have done—"

"Oh, shut up, Rick! What do you know about it? Stafford must try his luck, if he likes. Don't you fellows bother about him. I'll see him when he comes down."

"Would it be infernally uncivil if we happened to be out in the tandem!" suggested Rickmansworth.

"I expect he'd be rather glad."

"Then we will be out in the tandem. If you kill him, or the other way, just do it outside, will you, so as not to make a mess? Now we'll lunch, and then Bob, my boy, we'll evaporate."

It was about three o'clock when Stafford arrived. He had managed to catch the 1:30 from London, and must have started the moment he had read his letter. He was shown into the billiard-room, where Eugene was restlessly smoking a cigar.

He came swiftly up, and held out his hand, saying:

"This is like you, my dear old fellow. Not another man in England would have done it."

"Nonsense!" replied Eugene. "I ought to have done more."

"More? How?"

"I ought to have waited till you came before I went to see her."

"No, no; that would have been too much."

He was quite calm and cool; apparently there was nothing on his mind, and he spoke of Eugene's visit as if it concerned him little.

"I daresay you're surprised at all this," he continued, "but I can't talk about that now. It would upset me again. Beside, there's no time."

"Why no time?"

"I must go straight over and see her."

"My dear Charley, are you set on going?"

"Of course. I came for that purpose. You know how sorry I am we are rivals; but I agree with what you said—we needn't be enemies."

"It wasn't that I meant. But you don't ask how I fared."

"Well, I was expecting you would tell me, if there was anything to tell."

"I went, you know, to ask her to be my wife."

Stafford nodded.

"Well, did you?"

"No, not exactly."

"I thought not."

"I tried to—I mean I wasn't kept back by loyalty to you—you mustn't think that. But she wouldn't let me."

"I thought she wouldn't."

Eugene began to understand his state of mind. In another man such confidence would have made him angry; but he had only pity for Stafford.

"I must try and make him understand," he thought.

"Charley," he began, "I don't think you quite follow, and it's not very easy to explain. She didn't refuse me."

"Well, no, if you didn't ask," said Stafford, with a slight smile.

"And she didn't stop me in—in that way. Look here, old fellow; it's no use beating about the bush. I believe she means to have me."

Stafford said nothing.

"But I don't say that to put you off going, because I'm not sure. But I believe she does. And you ought to know what I think. I tell you all I know."

"Do you tell me not to go?"

"I can't do that. I only tell you what I believe."

"She said nothing of the sort?"

"No—nothing explicit."

"Merely declined to listen?"

"Yes—but in a way."

"My dear Eugene, aren't you deceiving yourself?"

"I think not. I think, you know, you're deceiving yourself."

They looked at one another, and suddenly both men smiled.

"I want to spare you," said Eugene; "but it sounds a little absurd."

"The sooner I go the better," said Stafford. "I must tell you, old fellow, I go in confident hope. If I am wrong—"

"Yes?"

"Everything is over! Would you feel that?"

Eugene was always honest with Stafford. He searched his heart.

"I should be cut up," he said. "But no—not that."

Stafford smiled sadly.

"How I wish I could do things by halves!" he exclaimed.

"You will come back?"

"I'll leave a line for you as I go by. Whatever happens, you have treated me well."

"Good-by, old man. I can't say good luck. When shall I see you?"

"That depends," said Stafford.

Eugene showed him the road to the Dower House, and he set out at a brisk walk.

CHAPTER XIII.

A Lover's Fate and a Friend's Counsel.

It was about half-past three when Stafford left Territon Park; about the same hour Claudia sallied forth from the Dower House to take her constitutional. When two people start to walk at the same time from opposite ends of the same road, barring accidents, they meet somewhere about the middle. In accordance with this law, when Claudia was about two miles from home, walking along the path through the dense woods of Territon Park, she saw Stafford coming toward her. There were no means of escape, and with a sigh of resignation she sat down on a rustic seat and awaited his approach. He saw her as soon as she saw him, and came up to her without any embarrassment.

"I am lucky," he said, "I was going over to see you."

Claudia had given some thought to this interview and had determined on her best course.

"Mr. Lane told me you were coming."

"Dear old Eugene!"

"But I hoped you would not."

"Don't let us begin at the end. I haven't seen you since I left Millstead. Were you surprised at my going?"

"I was rather surprised at the way you went."

"I thought you would understand it. Now, honestly, didn't you?"

"Perhaps I did."

"I thought so. You had seen what I only saw that very night. You understood —"

"Please, Father Stafford —"

"Say Mr. Stafford."

"No. I know you as Father Stafford, and I like that best."

"As you will—for the present. You knew how I stood. You saw I loved you—no, I am going on—and yet felt myself bound not to tell you."

"I saw nothing of the kind. It never entered my head."

"Claudia, is it possible? Did you never think of it?"

"As nothing more than a possibility—and a very unhappy possibility."

"Why unhappy?" he asked, and his voice was very tender.

"To begin with: you could never love any one."

"I have swept all that on one side. That is over."

"How can it be over? You had sworn."

"Yes; but it is over."

"Dare you break your vow?"

"If I dare, who else dare question me? Have I not counted the cost?"

"Nothing can make it right."

"Why talk of that? It is my sin and my concern."

"You destroy all my esteem for you."

"I ask for love, not for esteem. Esteem between you and me! I love you more than all the world."

"Ah! don't say that!"

"Yes, more than my soul. And you talk of esteem! Ah! you don't know what a man's love is."

"I never thought of you as making love."

"I think now of nothing else. Why should I trouble you with my struggles? Now I am free to love—and you, Claudia, are free to return my love."

"Did you think I was in love with you?"

"Yes," said Stafford. "But you knew my promise, and did not let yourself see your own feelings. Ah, Claudia! if it is only the promise!"

"It isn't only the promise. You have no right to speak like that. I should never have done as I did if I'd even thought of you like that."

"What do you mean by saying it's not only the promise?"

"Why, that I don't love you—I never did—oh, what a wretched thing!" And she rose and paced about, clasping her hands.

Stafford was very pale now, but very quiet.

"You never loved me?"

"No."

"But you will. You must, when you know my love—"

"No."

"Yes, but you will. Let me tell you what you are—"

"No, I never can."

"Is it true? Why?"

"Because—oh! don't you see?"

"No. Wasn't it because you loved me that you wouldn't let Eugene speak?"

"No, no, no!"

"Claudia," he cried, clasping her wrist, "were you playing with him?"

No answer seemed possible but the truth.

"Yes," she said, bowing her head.

"And playing with me?"

"No, that's unjust. I never did. I thought—"

"You thought I was beyond hurt?"

"I suppose so. You set up to be."

"Yes, I set up to be," he said bitterly.

"And the truth—in God's name let us have truth—is that you love him?"

"Have you no pity? Why do you press me?"

"I will not press you; God forbid I should trouble you! But is this the end?"

"Yes."

"It is final—no hope? Think what it means to me."

"If I do care for Mr. Lane, is this friendly to him?"

"I am beyond friendship, as I am beyond conscience. Claudia, turn to me. No man ever loved as I do."

"I can't help it," she said: "I can't help it!"

Stafford sank down on the seat and sat there for a moment without speaking. Claudia was awed at the look on his face.

"Don't look like that!" she cried. "You look like a man lost."

"Yes, lost!" he echoed. "All lost—all lost—and for nothing!"

Silence followed for a long time. Then he roused himself, and looked at her. Claudia's eyes were full of tears.

"It's not your fault, my sweet lady," he said gently. "You are pure and bright and beautiful, as you ever were, and I have raved and frightened you. Well, I will go."

"Go where?"

"Where? I don't know yet."

"I am so very, very sorry. But you must try—you must forget about it."

He smiled.

"Yes, I must forget about it."

"You will be yourself again—your old self—not weak like this, but giving others strength."

"Yes," he said again, humoring her.

"Surely you can do it—you who had such strength. And don't think hardly of me."

"I think of you as I used to think of God," he said; and bent and kissed her hand.

"Oh, hush!" she cried. "Pray don't!"

He kissed her hand once again, and then straightened himself, and said:

"Now I am going. You must forget—or remember Millstead, not Territon. And I—"

"Yes, and you?"

"I will go, too, where I may find forgetfulness. Good-by."

"Good-by," said Claudia, and gave him her hand again, her heart full of pity and almost of love. He turned on his heel, and she stood and watched him go. For a moment a sudden thought flashed through her head.

"Shall I call him back? Shall I ever find such love as his?"

She started a step forward, but stopped again.

"No, I do not love him," she said. "And I do love my careless Eugene. But God comfort him! O God, comfort him!"

And so standing and praying for him, she let him go.

And he went, with no falter in his step and never a look backward. This thing also had he set behind him.

Claudia still stood fixed on the spot where he had left her. Then she sat down on the seat, and gave herself up to memories of their walks and talks at Millstead.

"Why need he spoil it all?" she cried. "Why need he give me a sad memory, when I had such a pleasant one? Oh, how foolish they are! What a pity it's Eugene, and not him! Eugene would never have looked like that. He'd have made a bitter little speech, and then a pretty little speech, and smoothed his feathers and flown away. But still it is Eugene! Oh, dear, I shall never be quite happy again!"

We may reasonably, nay confidently, hope that this was looking at the black side of things. It is pleasant to act a little to ourselves now and then. The little pieces are thrilling, and they don't last much longer than their counterparts upon the stage. With most of us the curtain falls very punctually, leaving time for a merry supper, where we forget the headache and the thousand natural and unnatural ills that passed in our sight before the green baize let fall its merciful veil.

Stafford pursued his way through the woods. Arriving at the lodge gates, he stopped abruptly, remembering his promise to Eugene. He saw a little fellow playing about, and called to him.

"Do you know Mr. Lane, my boy?" he asked.

"Yes, sir," said the child.

"Then I'll give you something to take to him."

He took a card out of his pocket and wrote on it: "You were right. I am going to London"; and giving it, with a sixpence, to his messenger, resumed his journey to the station.

He was stunned. It cannot be denied that he had been blindly hopeful, blindly confident. He had persuaded himself that his love for Claudia could be nothing but the outcome of a natural bond between them that must produce a like feeling in her. He had attributed to her the depth and intensity of emotion that he found in himself. He had seen in her not merely a girl of more than common quickness, and perhaps more than common capacity, but a great nature ready to respond to a great passion in another. She had much to give to the man she loved; but Stafford asked even more than was hers to bestow. He had deceived himself, and the delusion was still upon him. He was conscious only of an utter, hopeless void. He had removed all to make room for Claudia, and Claudia refused to fill the vacant place. With all the will in the world she could not have filled it; but no such thought as this came to console Stafford. He saw his joy, but was forbidden to reach out his hand and pluck it. His life lay in the hollow of her hand, to grant or withhold, and she had closed her grasp upon it.

He did not rest until he reached his hotel, for he felt a longing to be able to sit down quietly and think it all over. He fancied that when he reached his own little room, the cloud that now seemed to hang over all his faculties would disperse, and he would see some plain road before him. In this he was not altogether disappointed, for it did become clear to him, as he sat in his chair, that the question he had to solve was whether he could now find any motive strong enough to keep him in life. He realized that Claudia's action must be accepted as a final destruction of his short dream of happiness. He felt that he could not go back to his old life, much less to his old attitude of mind, as if nothing had happened — as if he were an unchanged man, save for one sorrowful memory. The transformation had been too thorough for that. He had almost hoped that he would find himself the subject of some sudden revulsion of feeling, some uncontrollable fit of remorse, which would restore him, beaten and bruised, to his old refuge; but had his hope been realized, his sense of relief would, he knew, have been mingled with a measure of contempt for a mind so completely a prey to transient emotions. His nature was not of that sort, and he could not by a spasm of penitence nullify the events of the last few months. He must accept himself as altered by what he had gone through. Was there, then, any life left for the man he was now?

Undoubtedly, the easiest thing was to bid a quiet good-by to the life he had so mismanaged. He had never in old days been wedded to life. He had learnt always to regard it rather as a necessary evil than as a thing desirable in itself. Its momentary sweetness left it more bitter still. There would be a physical pang, inevitable to a strong man, full of health. But this he was ready to face; and now, in leaving life he would leave behind nothing he regretted. The religious condemnation of suicide, which in former days would not have decided, but prevented such a discussion in his mind, now weighed little with him. No doubt it would be an act of cowardice: but he had been guilty of such a much more flagrant treachery and desertion, that the added sin seemed a small matter. He felt that to boggle over it would be like condemning a murderer for trying to cheat the gallows. But still, there was the natural dislike of an acknowledgment of utter defeat; and, added to this, the bitter reluctance a man of ability feels at the idea of his powers ceasing to be active, and himself ceasing to be. The instinct of life was strong in him, though his reason seemed to tell him there was no way in which his life could be used.

"It's better to go!" he exclaimed at last, after long hours of conflicting meditation.

It was getting late in the evening. Eleven o'clock had struck, and he thought he would go to bed. He was very tired and worn out, and decided to put off further questions till the next day.

After all, there was no hurry. He knew the worst now; the blow had been struck, and only the dull, unending pain was with him—and would be till the hour came when he should free himself from it. He resolutely turned his mind away from Claudia. He could not bear to think about her. If only he could manage to think about nothing for an hour, sleep would come.

He rose to take his candle, but at the same moment a waiter opened the door.

"A gentleman to see you, sir."

"To see me? Who is it?"

"He says his name's Ayre, and he hopes you'll see him."

"I can't see him at this time of night," said Stafford, with the petulance of weariness. Why did the man bother him?

But Ayre had followed close on his messenger, and entered the room as Stafford spoke.

"Pray forgive me, Mr. Stafford," he said, "for intruding on you so unceremoniously."

Stafford received him with courtesy, but did not succeed in concealing his questioning as to the motive of the visit.

Ayre took the chair his host gave him.

"You think this a very strange proceeding on my part, I dare say?"

"How did you know I was here?"

"I had a wire from Eugene Lane. I'm afraid I seem to be taking a liberty, and that's a thing I hate doing. But I was most anxious to see you."

"Has Eugene any news?"

"What he says is this: It has happened as we feared. I am uneasy about him. Can you see him to-night?"

"I suppose, then, my fortune is known to you?"

"Yes; I wish I had seen you before you went. Do you mind my interfering?"

"No, not now. You could have done no good before."

"I could have told you it was no use."

"I shouldn't have believed you."

"I suppose you were bound to try it for yourself. Now, you think I don't understand your feelings."

"I suppose most people think they know how a man feels when he's crossed in love," said Stafford, trying to speak lightly.

"That's not the only thing with you."

"No, it isn't," he replied, a little surprised.

"I feel rather responsible for it all, you know. I was at the bottom of Morewood's showing you that picture."

"It must have dawned on me sooner of later."

"I don't know. But, yes—I expect so. You're hard hit."

Stafford smiled.

"Hard hit about her; and harder hit because it was a plunge to go into it at all."

"You're quite right."

"Of course I can't go into that side of it very much, but I think I know more or less how you feel."

"I really think you do. It surprises me."

"Yes. But, Stafford, may I go on taking liberties?"

"I believe you are my friend. Let us put that sort of question out of the way. Why have you come?"

"What does he mean by saying he's uneasy about you?"

"It's the old fellow's love for me."

Ayre was silent for a moment. Then he asked abruptly:

"What are you going to do?"

"I have hardly had time to look round yet."

"Why should it make any difference to you?"

Stafford was puzzled. He thought Ayre had really recognized the state of his mind. He was inclined to think so still. But how, then, could he ask such a question?

"You've had your holiday," Ayre went on calmly, "and a precious bad use you've made of it. Why not go back to work now?"

"As if nothing had happened?" This was the very suggestion he had made to himself, and scornfully rejected.

"You think you're utterly smashed, of course—I know what a facer it can be—and you're just the man to take it very hard. Stafford, I'm sorry." And with a sudden impulse he held out his hand.

Stafford grasped it. The sympathy almost broke him down. "She is all the world to me," he said.

"Aye, but be a man. You have your work to do."

"No, I have no work to do. I threw all that away."

"I expected you'd say that."

"I know, of course, what you think of it. In your view, that vow of mine was nonsense—a part of the high-falutin' way I took everything in. Isn't that so?"

"I didn't come here to try and persuade you to think as I do about such things. I am not so fond of my position that I need proselytize. But I want you to look into yours."

"Mine is only too clear. I have given up everything and got nothing. It's this way: all the heart is out of me. If I went back to my work I should be a sham."

"I don't see that. May I smoke?"

He lighted a cigar, and sat quiet for a few seconds.

"I suppose," he resumed, "you still believe what you used to teach?"

"Certainly; that is—yes, I believe it. But it isn't part of me as it was."

"Ah! but you think it's true?"

"I remain perfectly satisfied with the demonstration of its truth—only I have lost the faith that is above knowledge."

It was evidently only with an effort that Ayre repressed a sarcasm. Stafford saw his difficulty.

"You don't follow that?"

"I have heard it spoken of before. But, after all, it's beside the point. You believe the things so that, as far as honesty goes, you could still teach them?"

"Certainly I should believe every dogma I taught."

"Including the dogma that people ought to be good?"

"Including that," answered Stafford, with a smile.

"I don't see what more you want," said Sir Roderick, with an air of finality.

Stafford felt himself, against his will, growing more cheerful. In fact, it was a pleasure to him to exercise his brains once again, instead of being the slave of his emotions. Ayre had anticipated such a result from their conversation.

"Everything more," he said. "Personal holiness is at the bottom of it all."

"The best thing, I dare say." Ayre conceded. "But indispensable? Besides, you have it."

"Never again."

"Yes, I say—in all essentials."

"I can't do it. Ah, Ayre! it's all empty to me now."

"For God's sake, be a man! Is there nothing on earth to be but a saint or a husband?"

Stafford looked at him inquiringly.

"Heavens, man! have you no ambition? Here you are, with ten men's brains, and you sit—I don't know how you sit—in sackcloth, clearly, but whether for heaven or for Claudia I don't know. You think it odd to hear me preach ambition? I'm a lazy devil; but I have some power. Yes, I'm in my way a power. I might have been a greater. You might be a greater than ever I could."

Stafford listened.

"Do good if you can," Ayre went on, "and you can. But do something. Don't throw up the sponge because you had one fall. Make yourself something to live for."

"In the Church?"

"Yes—that suits you best. Your own Church or another. I've often wondered why you don't try the other."

"I've been very near trying it before now."

"It's a splendid field. Glorious! You might do anything."

Stafford was silent, and Ayre sat regarding him closely.

"Use my office for personal ambition?" he asked at last.

"Pray don't talk cant. Do some good work, and raise yourself high enough to do more."

"I doubt that motive."

"Never mind the motive. Do, man, do! and don't puke. Leave Eugene to lounge through life. He does it nicely. You're made for more."

Stafford looked up at him as he laid a hand on his shoulder.

"It's all misery," he said.

"Now, yes. But not always."

"And it's not what I meant."

"No, you meant to be a saint. Many of us do."

"I feel what you mean, but I have scruples."

Ayre looked at him curiously.

"You're not a man of scruples really," he said; "you'll get over them."

"Is that a compliment?"

"Depends on whom you ask. You'll think of it? Think of what you might do and be. Now, I'm off."

Stafford rose to show him out.

"I'm not sure whether I ought to thank you," he said.

"You will think of it?"

"Yes."

"And you won't kill yourself without seeing me again?"

"You were afraid of that?"

"Yes. Was I wrong?"

"No."

"You won't, then, without seeing me again?"

"No; I promise."

Ayre found his way downstairs, and into the street.

"It will work," he said to himself. "If the Humane Society did its duty, I should have a gold medal. I have saved a life to-night—and a life worth saving."

And Stafford, instead of going to bed, sat in his chair again, pondering the new things in his heart.

CHAPTER XIV.

Some People are as Fortunate as They Deserve to be.

Eugene Lane had been rather puzzled by Claudia's latest proceedings. On the morrow of her interview with Stafford he had received from her an incoherent note, in which she took great blame to herself for "this unhappy occurrence," and intimated that it would be long before she could bear to discuss any question pending between herself and her correspondent. Eugene was not disposed to acquiesce in this decision. He had done as much as honor and friendship demanded, and saw no reason why his own happiness should be longer delayed; for he had little doubt that Stafford's rebuff meant his own success. He could not, however, persist in seeking Claudia after her declaration of unwillingness to be sought; and he departed from Territon Park in some degree of dudgeon. All this sort of thing seemed to him to have a touch of the theater about it. But Claudia took it seriously; she did not forbid him to write to her, but she answered none of his letters, and Lord Rickmansworth, whom he encountered at one of the October race-meetings, gave him to understand that she was living a life of seclusion at Territon Park. Rickmansworth openly scoffed at this behavior, and Eugene did not know whether to be pleased at finding his views agreed with, or angry at hearing his mistress's whims treated with fraternal disrespect. Ultimately, he found himself, under the influence of lunch, coinciding with Rickmansworth's dictum that girls rather liked making fools of themselves, and that Claudia was no better than the rest. It was one of Eugene's misfortunes that he could not cherish illusions about his friends, unless his feeling toward Stafford must be ranked as an illusion. About the latter he had heard nothing, except for a short note from Sir Roderick, telling him that no tragedy of a violent character need now be feared. He was anxious to see Ayre and learn what passed, but that gentleman had also vanished to recruit at a German bath after his arduous labors.

It was mid-November before any progress was made in the matter. Eugene was in London, and so were very many people, for Parliament met in the autumn that year, and the season before

Christmas was more active than usual. He had met Haddington about the House, and congratulated him with a fervor and sincerity that had made the recipient of his blessings positively uneasy. Why should Lane be so uncommonly glad to get rid of Kate? thought the happy man who had won her from him. It really looked as if there were something more than met the eye. Eugene detected this idea in Haddington's mind, and it caused him keen amusement. Kate also he had encountered, and their meeting had been marked by the ceremonious friendship demanded by the circumstances. The flavor of diplomacy imparted to private life by these episodes had not, however, been strong enough to prevent Eugene being very bored. He was growing from day to day less patient of Claudia's invisibility, and he expressed his feeling very plainly one day to Rickmansworth, whom he happened to encounter in the outer lobby, as the noble lord was finding his way to the unwonted haunt of the House of Lords, thereto attracted by a debate on the proper precautions it behooved the nation to take against pleuro-pneumonia.

"Surprising," he said, "what interesting subjects the old buffers get hold of now and then! Come and hear 'em, old man."

"The Lord forbid!" said Eugene. "But I want to say a word to you, Rick, about Claudia. I can't stand this much longer."

"I wouldn't," said Rickmansworth, "if I were you; but it isn't my fault."

"It's absurd treating me like this because of Stafford's affair."

"Well, why don't you go and call in Grosvenor Square? She's there with Aunt Julia."

"I will. Do you think she'll see me?"

"My dear fellow, I don't know; only if I wanted to see a girl, I bet she'd see me."

Eugene smiled at his friend's indomitable self-confidence, and let him fly to the arms of pleuro-pneumonia. He then dispensed with his own presence in his branch of the Legislature, and took his way toward Grosvenor Square, where Lord Rickmansworth's town house was.

Lady Claudia was not at home. She had gone with her aunt earlier in the day to give Mr. Morewood a sitting. Mr. Morewood was painting her portrait.

"I expect they've stayed to tea. I haven't seen old Morewood for no end of a time. Gad! I'll go to tea."

And he got into a hansom and went, wondering with some amusement how Claudia had persuaded Morewood to paint her. It turned out, however, that the transaction was of a purely commercial character. Rickmansworth, having been very successful at the race-meeting above referred to, had been minded to give his sister a present, and she had chosen her own head on a canvas. The price offered was such that Morewood could not refuse; but he had in the course of the sitting greatly annoyed Claudia by mentioning incidentally that her face did not interest him and was, in fact, such a face as he would never have painted but for the pressure of penury.

"Why doesn't it interest you?" asked she, in pardonable irritation.

"I don't know. It's—but I dare say it's my fault," he replied, in that tone which clearly implies the opposite of what is asserted.

"It must be, I think," said Claudia gently. "You see, it interests so many people, Mr. Morewood."

"Not artists."

"Dear me! no!"

"Whom, then?"

"Oh, the nobility and gentry."

"And clergy?"

A shadow passed across her face—but a fleeting shadow.

"You paint very slowly," she said.

"I do when I am not inspired. I hate painting young women."

"Oh! Why?"

"They're not meant to be painted; they're meant to be kissed."

"Does the one exclude the other?"

"That's for you to say," said Morewood, with a grin.

"I think they're meant to be painted by some people, and kissed by other people. Let the cobbler stick to his last, Mr. Morewood."

"I wonder if you'll stick to your last," said Morewood.

Claudia decided that she had better not see this joke, if the contemptible quip could be so called. It was very impertinent, and she had no retort ready. She revenged herself by declaring her sitting at an end, and inviting herself and her aunt to stay to tea.

"I've got no end of work to do," Morewood protested.

"Surely tea is *compris*?" she asked, with raised eyebrows. "We shan't stay more than an hour."

Morewood groaned, but ordered tea. After all, it was too dark to paint, and—well, she was amusing.

Eugene arrived almost at the same moment as tea. Morewood was glad to see him, and went as near showing it as he ever did. Lady Julia received him with effusion, Claudia with dignity.

"I have pursued you from Grosvenor Square, Lady Julia," he said. "I didn't come to see old Morewood, you know."

"As much as to see me, I dare say," said Lady Julia in an aside.

Eugene protested with a shake of the head, and Morewood carried him off to have such inspection of the picture as artificial light could afford.

"You've got her very well."

"Yes, pretty well. It's a bright little shallow face."

"Go to the devil!" said Eugene, in strong indignation.

"I only said that to draw you. There is something in the girl—but not overmuch, you know."

"There's all I want."

"Oh, I should think so! Heard anything of Stafford?"

"No, except that he's gone off somewhere alone again. He wrote to Ayre; Ayre told me. He and Ayre are very thick now."

"A queer combination."

"Yes. I wonder what they'll make of one another!"

Morewood was a good-natured man at bottom, and after a few minutes' more talk he carried off Aunt Julia to look at his etchings.

"So I have run you down at last?" said Eugene to Claudia.

"I told you I didn't want to see you."

"I know. But that was a month ago."

"I was very much upset."

"So was I, awfully!"

"Do you think it was my fault, Mr. Lane?"

"Not a bit. So far as it was anybody's fault, it was mine."

"How yours?"

"Well, you see, he thought—"

"Yes, I see. You needn't go on. He thought you were out of the question, and therefore—"

"Now, Lady Claudia, are you going to quarrel again?"

"No, I don't think so. Only you are so annoying. Is he in great trouble?"

"He was. I think he's better now. But it was a terrible blow to him, as it would be to any one."

"To you?"

"It would be death!"

"Nonsense!" said Claudia. "What is he going to do?"

"I don't know. I think he will go back to work."

"I never intended any harm."

"You never do."

"You mean I do it? Pray don't try to be desperate and romantic, Mr. Lane. It's not in your line."

"It's curious I can never get credit for deep feeling. I have spent a miserable month."

"So have I."

"Because I could not see the person I love best in the world."

"Ah! that wasn't my reason."

"Claudia, you must give me an answer."

Claudia rose, and joined her aunt and Morewood. She gave Eugene no further opportunity for private conversation, and soon after the ladies took their leave. As Eugene shook hands with Claudia, he said:

"May I call to-morrow?"

"You are a little unkind; but you may." And she rapidly passed on to Morewood, and with much sparring made an appointment for her next sitting.

"Why does she fence so with me?" he asked the painter, as he took his hat.

"What's the harm? You know you enjoy it."

155

"I don't."

But it is very possible he did.

The next day Eugene took advantage of Claudia's permission. He went to Grosvenor Square, and asked boldly for Lady Claudia. He was shown into the drawing-room. After a time Claudia came to him.

"I have come for my answer," he said, taking her hand.

Claudia was looking grave.

"You know the answer," she said. "It must be 'Yes.'"

Eugene drew her to him and kissed her.

"But you say 'Yes' as if it gave you pain."

"So it does, in a way."

"You don't like being conquered even by your own prisoner?"

"It's not that; that is, I think, rather a namby-pamby feeling. At any rate, I don't feel it."

"What is it, then? You don't care enough for me?"

"Ah, I care too much!" she cried. "Eugene, I wish I could have loved Father Stafford, and not you."

"Why so?"

"I was at the very center of his life. I don't think I am more than on the fringe of yours."

"A very priceless fringe to a very worthless fabric!" said he, kissing her hand.

"Yes," she answered, with a smile, "you are perfect in that. You might give lessons in amatory deportment."

"Out of a full heart the mouth speaketh."

"Ah! does it? May not a lover be too *point-de-vice* in his speeches as well as in his accouterments? Father Stafford came to me pale, yes, trembling, and with rugged words."

"I am not the man that Stafford is—save for my lady's favor."

"And you came in confidence?"

"You had let me hope."

"You have known it for a long while. I don't trust you, you know, but I must. Will you treat me as you treated Kate?"

"Slander!" cried he gayly. "I didn't 'treat' Kate. Kate 'treated' me."

"Poor fellow!"

He had sat down in a low chair close to hers, and she bent down and kissed him on the forehead.

"At least, I don't think you'll like any one better than you like me, and I must be content with that."

"I have worshiped you for years. Was ever beauty so exacting?"

"With lucid intervals?"

"Never a moment. A sense of duty once led me astray—dynastic considerations—a suitable cousin."

"Yes; and I suppose a moonlight night."

"*Pereant quae ante te!* You know a little Latin?"

"I think I'd better not just now."

"You may want it for yourself, you know, with a change of gender. But we'll not bandy recriminations."

"I wasn't joking."

"Not when you began; but with me all your troubles shall end in jokes, and every tear in a smile. Claudia, I never knew you so alarmingly serious before."

"Well, I won't be serious any more. The fatal deed is done!"

"And I may say 'Claudia' now without fear of any one?"

"You will be able to say it for about the next fifty years. I hope you won't get tired of it. Eugene, try to get tired of me last of all."

"Never while I live! You are a perpetual refreshment."

"A lofty function!"

"And the spring of all my life. Let us be happy, dear, and never mind fifty years hence."

"I will," she said; "and I am happy."

"And, please God, you shall always be so. One would think it was a very dangerous thing to marry me!"

"I will brave the danger."

"There is none. I have found my goddess."

The door opened suddenly, and Bob Territon entered at the very moment when Eugene was sealing his vow of homage. Bob was pleased to be playful. Holding his hands before his face, he turned and pretended to fly.

"Come in, old man," cried Eugene, "and congratulate me!"

"Oh! you have fixed it, have you?"

"We have. Don't you think we shall do very well together?"

Bob stood regarding them, his hands in his pockets.

"Yes," he said at length, "I think you will. There's a pair of you."

And he could never be persuaded to explain this utterance. But it is to be feared that the thought underlying it was one not over-complimentary to the happy lovers. And Bob knew them both very well.

CHAPTER XV.

An End and a Beginning.

When Sir Roderick Ayre returned to England, he had to undergo much questioning concerning his dealings with Stafford. It had somehow become known throughout the little group of people interested in Stafford's abortive love-affair that he and Ayre had held conference together, and the impression was that Ayre's counsel had, to some extent at least, shaped Stafford's resolution and conduct. Ayre did not talk freely on the matter. He fenced with the idle inquiries of the Territon brothers; he calmed Mrs. Lane's solicitude with soothing words; he put Morewood off with a sneer at the transitoriness of love-affairs in general. To Eugene he spoke more openly, and did not hesitate to congratulate himself on the part he had taken in reconciling Stafford to life and work. Eugene cordially agreed with his point of view; and Ayre felt that he was in a fair way to be rid of the matter, when one day Claudia sprang upon him with a new assault.

He had come to see her, and tender hearty congratulations. He felt that the successful issue of Eugene's suit was in some degree his own work, and he was well pleased that his two favorites should have taken to one another. Moreover, he reaped intellectual satisfaction from the fulfillment of a prophecy made when its prospect of realization seemed very scant. Claudia admitted her own pleasure in her engagement, and did not attempt to deny that her affection had dated from a period when by all the canons of propriety she should have had no thoughts of Eugene.

"We are not responsible for our emotions," she said, laughing; "and you will admit I behaved with the utmost decorum."

"About your usual decorum," he replied. "The situation was difficult."

"It was indeed," she sighed. "Eugene was so very—well, reckless. But I want to ask you something."

"Say on."

"I heard about your interview with Father Stafford; what did you say to him?"

"Of course Eugene has told you all I told him?"

"Probably. I told him to."

"Well, that's all."

"In fact, you told him I wasn't worth fretting about!"

"Not in that personal way. I asserted a general principle, and reluctantly denied that you were an exception."

"I hope you did tell him I wasn't worth it, and very plainly. But hasn't he gone back to his religious work?"

"I think he will."

"Did you advise him to do that?"

"Yes, certainly. It's what he's most fit for, and I told him so."

"He spoke to me as if—as if he had no religion left."

"Yes, it took him in that way. He'll get over that."

"I think you were wrong to tell him to go back. Didn't you encourage him to go back to the work without feeling the religion?"

"Perhaps I did. Did Eugene tell you that?"

"Yes."

"I'll never say anything to a lover again."

"Didn't you tell him to use his work for personal ends—for ambition, and so on?"

"Oh, in a way. I had to stir him up—I had to tide him over a bad hour."

"That was very wrong. It was teaching him to degrade himself."

"He can pursue his work in perfect sincerity. I found that out."

"Can he if he does it with a low motive?"

"My dear girl, whose motives are not mixed? Whose heart is single?

"His was once!"

"Before he met—you and me? I made the best job I could. I cemented the breakage; I couldn't undo it."

"I would rather—"

"He'd picturesquely drown himself?"

"Oh, no," she said, with a shudder; "but it lowers my ideal of him."

"That, considering your position, is not wholly a bad thing."

"Do you think he's justified in doing it?"

"To tell the truth, I don't see quite to the bottom of him. But he will do great things."

"Now he is well quit of me?"

Sir Roderick smiled.

"Well, I don't like it."

"Then you should have married him, and left Eugene to do the drowning."

"Do you know, Sir Roderick, I rather doubt if Eugene would have drowned himself?"

"I don't know; he has very good manners."

They both laughed.

"But all the same, I am unhappy about Mr. Stafford."

"Ah, your notions of other people's morality are too exalted. I don't accept responsibility for Stafford. He would not have followed my suggestion unless the idea had been in germ in his own mind."

Claudia's pre-occupation with Stafford's fate would have been somewhat disturbing to a lover less philosophical or less sympathetic than Eugene. As it was, he was pleased with her concern, and his sorrow for the trouble it occasioned her was mitigated by a conviction that its effect would not be permanent. In this idea he proved perfectly correct. As the weeks passed by and nothing was heard of the vanished man, his place in the lives of those who had been so intimately associated with him became filled with other interests, and from a living presence he dwindled to an occasional memory. It was as if he had really died. His name was now and then mentioned with the sad affection we accord to those who have gone before us; for the most part the thought of him was thrust out in the busy give-and-take of everyday life. Save for the absence of that bitter sense of hopelessness which the separation of death brings, Stafford might as well have passed on the road which, but for Ayre's intervention, he had marked out for himself. Claudia and Eugene were wrapped up in one another; their love tor him, though not dead, was dormant, and his name was oftener upon the lips of Ayre and Morewood than of those who had been most closely united with him in the bonds of common experience. But Ayre and Morewood, besides entertaining a kindly memory of his personal charm, found delight in studying him as a problem. They were keenly interested in the upshot of his new start in life, and their blunter perceptions were deaf to the dissonance between the ideal he had set before himself and the alternative Ayre had suggested for his adoption. Perhaps they were right. If none but saints may do the work of the world, much of its most useful work must go undone.

Haddington and Kate Bernard were married before Christmas. Claudia deprecated such haste; and Eugene willingly acquiesced in her wish to put off the date of their own union. He thought that being engaged to Claudia was a pleasant state of existence, and why hasten to change it? Besides, as he suggested, they were not people of fickle mind, like Kate and Haddington (for, of course, Claudia had told him of Haddington's proposal to herself—it is believed ladies always do tell these incidents), and could afford to wait. Eugene went to the wedding. He was strongly opposed to such foolish things as standing quarrels, and Kate was entirely charming in the capacity of somebody else's wife: it is a comparatively easy part to fill, and he had no fault to find with her conception of it. The magnificence of his wedding present smoothed his return to favor, and Kate had the good sense to accept the *rôle* he offered her, and allowed it to be supposed that she had been the faithless, he the forsaken, one; whereas in reality, as Ayre remarked, she had herself doubled the parts. Claudia judiciously avoided the question of her presence at the ceremony by a timely absence from London, and enjoyed only at second-hand the amusement Eugene derived from Haddington's hesitation between triumph over his supposed rival, and doubt, which had in reality gained the better part. In spite of this doubt, it is allowable to hope for a very fair share of working happiness in the Haddington household. Kate was hardly a woman to make a man happy; but, on the other hand, she would not prevent him being happy if his bent lay in that direction. And Haddington was too entirely contented with himself to be other than happy.

Eugene's wedding was fixed for the Easter recess, and among the party gathered for the occasion at Millstead were most of those who had been his guests in the previous summer. The Haddingtons were not there—Kate retorted Claudia's evasion; and of course Stafford's figure was missing; but the Territon brothers were there, and Morewood and Ayre, the former bringing with him the completed picture, which was Rickmansworth's present to his sister. The party was to be enlarged the day before, the wedding by a large company of relations of both their houses.

The evening before this invasion was expected, Eugene came down to dinner looking rather perturbed. He was a little silent during the meal, and when the ladies withdrew, he turned at once to Ayre:

"I have heard from Stafford."

"Ah! what does he say?"

"He has joined the Church of Rome."

"I thought he would."

Morewood grunted angrily.

"Did you tell him to?" he asked Ayre.

"No; I think I referred to it."

"Do you suppose he's honest?" Morewood went on.

"Why not?" asked Eugene. "I could never make out why he didn't go before. What do you say, Ayre?"

Sir Roderick was a little troubled. This exact following of, or anyhow coincidence with, his advice seemed to cast a responsibility upon him.

"Oh, I expect he's honest enough; and it's a splendid field for him," he answered, repeating the argument he had urged to Stafford himself.

"Ayre," said Morewood aggressively, "you've driven that young man to perdition."

"Bosh!" said Ayre. "He's not a sheep to be driven, and Rome isn't perdition. I did no more than give his thoughts a turn."

"I think I am glad," said Eugene; "it is much better in some ways. But he must have gone through another struggle, poor fellow!"

"I doubt it," said Ayre.

"Anyhow, it's rather a score for those chaps," remarked Rickmansworth. "He's a good fish to land."

"Yes, it will make a bit of a sensation," assented Ayre. "We'll see what the Bishop says when he comes to turn Eugene off. By the way, is it public property?"

"It will be in the papers, I expect, to-morrow. I wonder what they'll say!"

"Everything but the truth."

"By Jove, I hope so. And we alone know the secret history!"

"Yes," said Ayre; "and you, Rick, will have to sit silent and hear the enemy triumph."

Lord Rickmansworth did not think it worth while to repudiate the *odium theologicum* imputed to him. Probably he knew he was in reality above the suspicion of caring for such things.

"Shall you tell Claudia?" Ayre asked Eugene, as they went upstairs.

"Yes; I shall show her his letter. I think I ought, don't you?"

"Perhaps; will you show it me?"

"Yes; in fact he asks me to give you the news, as he is too occupied to write to you. The note is quite short, and, I think, studiously reserved."

He gave it to Ayre, who read it silently. It ran:

"DEAR EUGENE:

"A line to wish Lady Claudia and yourself all happiness and joy. Do not let your joy be shadowed by over-kind thoughts of me. I am my own man again. You will see soon by the papers that I have taken the important step of being received into the Catholic Church. I need not trouble you with an argument. I think I have done well, and hope to find there work for my hands to do. Pray give this news to Ayre, and with it my most warm and friendly remembrances. I would write but for my stress of work. He was a friend to me in my need. They are sending me to Rome for a time; after that I hope I shall come to England, and renew my friendships. Good-by, old fellow, till then. I long for ἧστ᾽ ἀγαυοφροςύη καὶ σοῖς ἀγανῖς ἐπέεσσιν.

"Yours always,

"C.S.K."

"That doesn't tell one much, does it?"

"No," said Ayre; "but we shall learn more if we watch him."

Claudia came up, and they gave her the note to read.

She read it, asking to have the Greek translated to her. Then she said to Ayre:

"What does it mean?"

"Why do you ask me?"

"Because you are most likely to know."

"Mind, I may be wrong; I may do him injustice, but I think —"

"Yes?" she said impatiently.

"I think, Lady Claudia, you have spoilt a Saint and made a Cardinal!"